A PERFECT FAMILY

SARAH SHERIDAN

The right of Sarah Sheridan to be identified as the Author of the Work has been
asserted by her in accordance with the Copyright, Designs and Patents Act 1988.
First published in 2022 by Bloodhound Books.

www.bloodhoundbooks.com

Print ISBN 978-1-5040-7254-0

ALSO BY SARAH SHERIDAN

For my amazing cousin, Kate

CHAPTER ONE

I t was Saturday morning when we found the bodies. They were just hanging there, all six of them. At first, I thought it was a joke; I fleetingly wondered if one of the kids had stuffed some old clothes together to make them look human, and then strung them up from the conservatory roof. It was just a week away from Halloween, so that was my first thought; that someone in the family was getting the decorations ready early. But that was when I hadn't fully walked through the kitchen door and onto the cool marble slabs, when I'd just glanced up and first caught sight of the bodies. Because what normal person goes into a house expecting to find the whole family who lives in it dead? I certainly didn't, and neither did Jack. Poor Jack; however bad it was for me to see all but one of the Bryant clan grey and strung up like meat in a butcher's, what must it have been like for their only surviving immediate family member to walk into a scene like that? To see his mother, grandmother, sisters and brother suspended from the ceiling of the conservatory – the usually cosy and comfortable extension at the back of the house – hanging from the poles that his mum, Penelope Bryant, had fitted so that she could hang fairy lights around the room? Jesus, the word nightmare barely scratches the surface of the horrific, gruesome discovery that we made. Of the hellish darkness that immediately flooded our minds. Jack was behind me, he was second to realise what was going on. And the whimpering noise that he made as he went down to the floor struck a sadness into my heart that I've never felt before.

As I bent down to stroke my best friend's hair, to try to soothe him – although I knew no one would ever be able to take away the pain that had suddenly been thrust upon him – a strange calmness came over me. As my mum tells anyone who will listen; I'm usually a drama queen. I don't like spiders, or the dark, or blood, or arguments. I go to pieces if I watch sad films, and I have to leave the room if my brother – Tom – starts watching that true crime stuff that he likes. That was when he lived with us, before he went to the boarding school for kids with anger problems. I'd never have thought I'd be able to deal with the situation that I found myself in that morning, but I did. I kept stroking Jack's hair with one hand, and reached into my jacket pocket for my phone with the other one. I dialled the three nines, and calmly asked the operator to connect me to the police. I explained what had happened, and my voice sounded steady and firm when it came out. I didn't cry or scream, and when I told my mum all about this later, she said she was very proud of me, and that I must have hidden inner strengths. I've since found that I have a lot of them; I haven't had a choice in that, not with everything that happened next.

It wasn't long before two police cars and an ambulance parked up outside the Bryants' large house. In the minutes between phoning the police and waiting for them to arrive, I'd managed to move Jack away from the conservatory, and had half-walked, half-dragged him back to the front room. I figured that there was no point in us looking at his hanging family members any longer. He curled up on the carpet in the living room as soon as we entered it, and was shaking uncontrollably in the foetal position as I hugged him and waited for the emergency services to arrive. My strange, almost out-of-body calmness continued, which was a relief. I saw the blue lights through the window from my kneeling position on the rug, and immediately stood up.

'I'll be back in a minute, Jack,' I said. 'There are people here who can help us now. Okay?'

I heard Jack groan as I left the room and went to open the front door.

A uniformed officer was standing there, with two paramedics beside him.

'Hello, I'm DS Moretti,' the tall police officer said, stepping forwards. He had a very deep, raspy voice. 'Can you show us what's been going on here, please?'

Seconds later, we were all standing in the conservatory. Not Jack though, he was still on the living room floor. It broke my heart to think of the pain he must have been feeling at that moment, I desperately wanted to be with him, but I had to show the emergency services people the bodies. As they took in the horrific scene, the sickening sight of the dead people – particularly the two smaller ones – the two paramedics only paused for a few seconds before their professionalism kicked in and they started attending to each body in turn. I imagined that they didn't get a call like this very regularly; I'd never have been able to imagine something so awful if I hadn't seen it with my own eyes. I couldn't properly focus on anything else in the room; the bodies were everything, the spectacle of them made everything seem oddly unreal, like I was in a movie that had come to life. I moved to the side to let one of the paramedics past, and almost fell over a stool, which then fell on top of a pile of notebooks.

'They're looking for signs of life,' DS Moretti said. He hadn't taken his eyes off the bodies since entering the room.

'All deceased.' The female paramedic turned towards him.

'Right,' DS Moretti said, as his hand went into his pocket. I watched as he withdrew his mobile phone and tapped the screen a few times.

'Sarge,' he said into it a few seconds later. 'I think you're going to want to come and take a look at this. We've got six dead bodies here. And at the moment, I'm not sure whether it's suicide or murder.'

CHAPTER TWO

J ack and I have known each other since we were six years old. I'm two years younger than him, and to start with I was friends with his younger sister, Sabrina. We were in the same year at St Giles Primary School in Buckingham, and when I was six, Sabrina invited me round to her house for the first time. She had bright blonde hair, like the rest of the family, and I thought it looked amazing; my hair's always been copper brown, and I used to wonder what it felt like to look like Sabrina. She had delicate features, even when she was young.

'Elfin', my mother used to say. 'She looks like a changeling; she's got the body and face of a fairy.'

It was the day after my eighteenth birthday when we found the bodies of his family, and I will never get over seeing Sabrina hanging there like that, her mouth all contorted, her eyes blindfolded, her limbs unnaturally stiff, her skin the colour of death. She didn't deserve to have her life cut short like that, she had so much going for her; everybody said so. Some horrors in life are literally indescribable, and that is one of them. I'll never get over what I saw that day.

My family have always been boringly normal. I used to

want a more interesting name, as I figured that 'Ellen Waldron' wasn't going to get me very far in life. It sounds more like a librarian sort of name than a go-getting success-story kind of title. I've always loved reading, and I would ponder over girls' names in stories like Scarlett, Anastasia, Mathilda, Evangeline and Ramona, and wonder if my classmates would find me a bit more interesting if I was called something more exotic. Perhaps a more memorable name would have counteracted my overall averageness; I had average looks, an average-sized body, average marks in classes; I was about the most boringly 'normal' girl you could get. And until I was twelve, I came from an average family. Then my father left, because it turned out that he'd been having an affair behind my mum's back with a lady from church, and when he left our household, everything changed. I haven't seen my dad much since; he used to come and take my little brother and I out to restaurants or the bowling alley shortly after he left, but I always found these meetings with him a bit awkward and they've petered out over the years, although I do speak to him on the phone from time to time. My brother still has a love–hate relationship with him; he needs his dad, but he detests how he treated our mum. He had to stop his irregular meetups with him because he was getting so angry he used to trash our house, and his classroom at school. In the end, after he was expelled, my mum found him a place at a special boarding school that helps kids that have emotional and behavioural challenges like his. My mum has always done her best with me and my brother, bless her, but she's still sad most of the time. It's like my dad's departure catapulted her into a depression that she's never been able to shake off. And she's too bloody stubborn to go to the doctor and ask for help; if I try to talk to her about her low moods she just says she's fine. 'I'm okay, Ellen, really. I don't know why you keep bringing this subject up.' So I just end up leaving it alone and letting her get on with staring into space while her tea stews on the sideboard.

The one nice thing my dad has done for me in recent years, is give me the run of his mum's old flat near Buckingham University. When I started my sociology degree, I was still living at home – my mum's house is a twenty minute walk from the uni. But my brother's anger – and then departure – and my mum's near-constant mild depression was getting to me, and I just felt like I needed to be somewhere else so I could emotionally breathe. I told my dad a bit about this when we were talking on the phone one day, and he said that the tenants had moved out of his mum's (Granny's) old flat – she's been dead eight years now, bless her – and would I like to stay there for a bit by myself? I jumped at the chance, although Mum wasn't happy about it to start with. I inherited the previous tenants' cat along with the flat, apparently they'd just left her there and hadn't provided a forwarding address. So I named her Nala – I've always loved *The Lion King* – and did my best to look after her. And it wasn't long before Jack moved into the spare bedroom. He also needed a break from his family, he said he had too many siblings, and that he was too old to be living with his mum anymore. He was a writer now, he said. He'd always been good with words, so I told him he would be very successful at his chosen trade one day. He said he needed some peace and quiet to think, and I totally understood this. We'd been in the flat together all Friday afternoon, evening and night – while his poor family were dying together in their conservatory. He'd bought me a birthday cake, and we'd sat on the sofa together and watched my favourite films back to back until we'd fallen asleep. It was exactly how I wanted to spend my birthday, just with my best friend. I've never been one to hold big parties or anything, although I've been to a few that my friends have held before. Personally, I prefer a film night in, if given the choice. I'd woken up at around four in the morning, stiff and uncomfortable on the sofa, and found that Jack had already taken himself off to bed. I glanced into his room on the way to mine, and could hear him snoring and see the shape of his body under his duvet. It was horrible to think that we were having such a good time, when his family was having such a bad one. If only we'd known, we would have moved heaven and earth to help them...

I did have a couple of friends in school before Sabrina arrived – Jane and Kim – but we were never that close. We rarely went round to each other's houses after school or at the weekends, or things like that. When Sabrina joined St Giles School I was mesmerised by her immediately. Even though I was only little, I remember having the sensations of wonderment and excitement as I watched her enter our colourful little classroom for the first time. She seemed so self-contained and confident, and she was very striking to look at. Her lips were naturally bright red, her eyes the palest blue, her lashes long and her skinny frame held high and proud. After we'd been let out for our thirty minutes of exercise in the playground, all the girls immediately wanted to make friends with her that breaktime. But for some reason, Sabrina gravitated towards me; much to Kim and Jane's astonishment. I was overjoyed and astounded by her attention; I was usually the hanger-on, the frumpy extra in the background of friendship groups. But now here was the fascinating new girl making a beeline for me. Maybe she thought I looked like a steady person, a reliable kind of girl. I didn't care why she chose me. I wasn't about to argue, I was so happy. And it wasn't long before Sabrina's mum, Penelope, stopped mine at the school gates and asked if I'd like to come over for tea one afternoon. I was thrilled.

I soon found out that the rest of the Bryant family were just as exotically interesting as Sabrina, if not more. When I met them, they'd just moved into a huge house on the outskirts of Buckingham town. Sabrina's dad – Dalton – was still alive then, and as soon as I met him I realised where Sabrina and the other siblings had got their blonde hair from. Penelope had fair hair too, but it was more straw coloured, whereas their dad's shone like the sun. He was a giant of a man; tall and broad-shouldered with a ruddy face, freckles and sharp eyes, with a shock of white-blond hair on top of his head that stuck out at different angles. He was very much the dominant one in the house; Penelope, their mum, was like a calm, caring angel – at least that's what I thought back then – always baking delicious scones and cakes, or folding washing, or running around after the younger children making sure they'd done their homework.

Jack was up a tree in their huge garden when I met him for the first time. I found out that Penelope and Dalton had decided to send their boys to a private single-sex school for reasons I'd never fully understood, which is why I'd never seen him in the playground at St Giles School before. He had a cheeky, freckly face, the ubiquitous Bryant blond hair, and long, tanned limbs. He told me and Sabrina to go away when he saw us, as he said he was busy hiding from Samuel – their younger brother, who was only four at the time. Their little sister, Adele, was only two then, and Zara had yet to be born. I do remember how the children were always beautifully dressed back then, the girls in flowery dresses and the boys in shorts and shirts. After I got to know the Bryants, I started asking my mum to buy me skirts and dresses, rather than the practical tracksuits she seemed to favour. She used to roll her eyes a bit, but was kind enough to do as I'd asked.

'Very patriarchal household,' my mother said one day, as she drove me home from yet another play date with Sabrina. I remember watching her nose wrinkle as she said this, although I never understood what she really meant until years later. After my own father left, my mum became vaguely feminist. Not the marching, bra-burning type, more the literary version who would 'like' pro-women comments on Facebook. She hasn't ever had the emotional energy to take up any cause fully – not since Dad left anyway – but her desire for girls to have the same opportunities and treatment as boys has become more and more evident over the years. Perhaps because of their differing mindsets, Mum and Penelope never became particularly good friends. They would tolerate each other, and have the occasional cup of tea together, but that's as far as it went. But knowing what I now do about the Bryants, Penelope's reservations about getting really close to anyone outside her family are very understandable.

When I first got to know them, the Bryants seemed like a golden family to me. Everything from their striking looks, their glowing hair, their shiny, well-kept house, their happy natures and their polished manners seemed beyond perfect. Almost too good to be true. I've since learned that when a situation seems this way, when it's so perfect it makes you ache with jealousy inside, it's usually because it's a carefully constructed veneer, which might be hiding a plethora of secrets beneath its surface gloss. I was beyond shocked when the truth about the Bryants' real home life started to slowly filter through after Dalton's death due to a heart attack four years ago. I went to his funeral, it was a grand and solemn affair with more extended family members appearing than I ever knew Sabrina had. Most of them were formidable, stand-offish characters, and there was never any need for me to talk to them. I just remember Jack and Sabrina staring at their father's coffin as it was marched slowly down the aisle of the church, their faces white. *What must they be thinking?* I wondered. *Probably full of grief,* I'd decided at the time. That was before I knew what I do now, of course.

CHAPTER THREE

Poor Jack. Another piece broke away from my heart every time I looked at him that day; that awful Saturday when we found his family members' bodies. By the time the forensic people had arrived – all busy and professional in their white suits – he was half propped up, leaning against the sofa in the front room. It was like he'd become catatonic, and to be honest his behaviour was adding an extra layer of fear on top of the horror that I already felt. He'd stopped moaning by then, in fact he wasn't making any noise. He wouldn't even look at me when I asked him if he was okay. He just stared straight ahead, his eyes unblinking, his normally tanned skin pale. I thought he must be staring into something I couldn't see, brought on by the shock of finding his family dead like that. He looked like he was gazing straight into hell.

I heard a voice outside that I recognised.

'Oh God, Jack,' I said, taking my hand away from his and standing up. 'Your Aunt Marjorie's arrived.' I peered through the window. 'And your Uncle Patrick is with her.' My heart sunk as I watched these two formidable characters question the police officers who were barring their entrance to the house. I could now hear their raised voices from where I stood.

'Let us in this instant,' Marjorie was saying, her perfectly pronounced words clipped and shrill. 'This is my sister-in-law's house. We have a right to know what's going on here. You can't just keep us stuck outside like this. Go and get whoever is in charge here this instant.'

Marjorie was used to being obeyed, I thought, as I watched the police officer make placating gestures with his gloved hands. He didn't move from his spot in front of the house, which meant he obviously had no plans to go and find a superior for Marjorie to turn her wrath on to. I couldn't hear exactly what he was saying to her in reply, but his general tone sounded soothing. Police must be used to irate relatives turning up to crime scenes, I reflected. Not that Marjorie was having one bit of the officer's calm but firm refusal of her demands. After a final blast at him about her views on general police incompetency, she stopped berating him and turned towards the house.

'Penelope?' she called loudly. 'Jack? If any of you are in there, come outside immediately and let Patrick and I know what on earth is going on here. We've been worried to death ever since Mrs Parker called in and told us about the emergency vehicles parked outside your house.'

The Bryant clan was a much wider one than just their immediate family; a fact that I'd discovered quite soon after becoming friends with Sabrina. Many generations of Dalton's family had lived in Buckingham, and some of them seemed determined to keep this tradition going for as long as they could. Sabrina had told me that the only reason that her family had moved away was because of her dad's work. He did something important to do with money and was high up in some company. But that they had moved back as soon as they conceivably could, when Dalton was transferred back to the Milton Keynes office.

Sabrina tried to explain their family set-up to me once, describing what it was like to be one of many blonde-haired Bryants. She said that they were all expected to abide by an unwritten code of conduct that pervaded the family; this included being super polite to outsiders and to each other, and always being well turned out and respectable-looking. But most of all, she had to obey the head of her family, her father Dalton. His word was law in their household; he had the final say on everything. She said that he'd had to look up to his father in the same way. She described Dalton as being so sure of his own mind, that when their neighbour raised a dispute over the boundary fencing between their two properties, her dad was so incensed that the neighbour – Mr Coleman – had dared to question the validity of his property, that he had verbally torn shreds off the man while they stood together in the street, and that this outburst of her father's had mortified her. Apparently Mr Coleman now hated her family, but because her dad was a fine, upstanding, churchgoing man, most of the neighbours had chosen to turn a blind eye to his angry ranting and said no more about it. Sabrina said that once her father had been crossed and fallen out with someone, he never forgave them. She said that he and Marjorie never spoke to their older brother, Jacob, anymore. She didn't know why, but they'd fallen out with him years ago over something, and his name was now dirt in their household. After she'd told me that, Sabrina stopped talking and I noticed her cheeks flush purple. I wondered if she was thinking that she'd told me too much; that she regretted her unusual openness that day.

My thoughts were distracted by movement outside the window. I stared, as Marjorie leant over the fence towards the house.

'Penelope,' she shouted. 'Can you hear me?'

It was at that point that I caught the tail end of a

13

conversation between two police officers that was going on just outside the room I was in.

'Yes, that woman certainly is making herself known,' one of them was saying. 'Makes you wonder why. It's almost a bit too much of a show that she's putting on, do you know what I mean? Can't help wondering why she's drawing so much attention to herself. It doesn't seem quite right. I'll have a word with DS Moretti about bringing her to the station for a chat, because my gut feeling is telling me that we need to have a serious chat with her about what she might know about what's happened here...'

CHAPTER FOUR

How does this happen to such a perfect family? I wondered, over and over again, as I fought to keep the scene of the hanging bodies from my mind. There was no way I was going to leave Jack's side, but he wasn't speaking – couldn't say anything – so for the best part of several hours, I stayed silent too, except when the busy professionals asked me a question. Flashes from the past kept rolling through my thoughts; memories of better days. I remembered how well-dressed Penelope had been when I'd first met her; her clothes always looked so perfect on her slight frame. And she always knew the best thing to say in any situation; the most appropriately social thing to do. Dalton was a bit intimidating, but he was socially trained too, and they both seemed a breed apart to me; more exotic and refined than the 'normal' people I'd grown up with. Penelope didn't watch soap operas on TV, or complain about period pains, or swear when she burnt her hand in the oven, like my mum did. She was just constantly self-composed, almost like a mum from an old-fashioned film. Dalton always seemed to be busy doing something purposeful; gardening, mending something in the house, striding off to work. When he spoke, he said everything with such self-assuredness that when I was little I thought he must be the cleverest person alive; that he must know everything that there was to know. The pair of them were very different from my mum and dad; when my dad was living with us he was generally out having a beer at the pub with his mates when I was young, or when he was at home, he liked watching the rugby while swearing at the television. My mum seemed much less sure of herself than Penelope; she was always asking how I was, or worrying about me, or feeling tired, or forgetting something from her shopping list. Dalton and Penelope seemed to have evolved past these type of things, to an existence more meaningful and perfect. At least, that's how it seemed to me when I was little.

Their children seemed to have inherited their parents' gift for self-contained confidence. Whereas I was always questioning who I was, or what I was doing, or how I was coming across to people; Sabrina, Jack and their siblings simply were *themselves* at all times. They never seemed to worry about the things that I did. They just had complete confidence in who they were and what they were doing. My mum called this entitlement; as I got older I called it self-assurance; and I wanted a piece of it. I tried to act like Sabrina and the rest of them, but that's all I managed; acting. I never felt as confident as them. I would try out different poses and sentences at school, trying to become so confident that I would eventually stop worrying about being confident, but it never happened. I would always rake over things afterwards, and wonder how on earth the Bryant children managed to be like they were on a daily basis.

But knowing what I know now, I can't help wondering if the Bryants were taking on even greater acting roles than I was. What if I was more genuine than them back then?

CHAPTER FIVE

I stayed with Jack for hours, stroking his hair and whispering comforting things to him. Food and drink were of no concern to us at that time, although at one point a nice police officer did bring us both a tea in a paper cup. She asked if we wanted a sandwich, but I shook my head. I wasn't sure I'd ever be able to eat again, and Jack couldn't even talk at that point, let alone consume any food.

'I'm sorry, I can't move him,' I said to one of the forensic team who'd come into the house, and stared at Jack with mild irritation. 'He just needs to be here, I think. He's finding it so hard to process what we saw this morning.'

The man had nodded, and then gone about his business.

I watched as the forensic people came in and out, as the detectives prowled around, and as the uniformed police officers lined the outside of the house. Quite a crowd was gathering outside by then, including some media crews. Word travels fast around a small town like Buckingham, and a tragedy or crime of this size would never stay hidden for very long. I could only remember one death being reported around here in the recent past, and that was the mysterious murder of an old man up the road in Maids Moreton. Things like this just didn't happen in Buckingham, or anywhere else in the world, as far as I knew. The whole thing was insanely awful. I just wanted everyone to go away; it was all so overwhelming.

It was late afternoon by the time I finally walked through my mum's front door, and sank into her arms. I breathed in her familiar, lavender soap scent; never in my life had I been so glad to smell it. I knew I couldn't go back to my flat for a while; there was no way that I could be on my own at that point. The huge weight of everything – that I'd been squashing down because I'd needed to look after Jack, making sure that he was surviving the ordeal – finally erupted out of me, and I sobbed uncontrollably into my mum's shoulder for a good ten minutes. Being near her was soothing in itself, and I felt the pressure of everything that had happened lifting off me a teeny tiny bit. The detective had questioned me for ages, and had asked me about where me and Jack had been over the last forty-eight hours. I'd been completely honest, and had told him that it had been my birthday the day before, and that we'd been together all day, evening and night watching films. I told him how I'd posted snaps of this on my Facebook account, and even pulled my phone out to show him. There were several nice ones of me, Jack and Nala the cat cuddled up together. I said that I'd known Jack had been there all night because at one point after I'd fallen asleep on the sofa, and had got up to go to my bed, he'd been snoring away in his. And the thought of him having anything to do with his family's demise was absolutely ludicrous anyway. I mean, I know the police have a job to do, and they have to question the people closest to the victims first whenever anything awful happened, but Jack was honestly the least violent person I knew. He was just a big softy. So I told the detective about what a lovely person Jack was, and how he was my best friend, and that I trusted him with my life. And how caring he'd always been to his siblings, in all the years that I'd known him. That's why he was in bits now, I explained. Because his whole family being wiped out like this is his worst nightmare. It's anyone's worst nightmare, come to that.

DS Moretti had then tried to talk to Jack – but in vain. No one could get a word out of him, he was incapable of doing anything, and in the end I'd had to ask them to leave him alone, and try to talk to him another day. The whole thing had been like the worst waking dream you could imagine. I honestly couldn't believe it had all happened. I'd had to be so strong, so in control, in a situation that had been absolutely unbearable. It was too much. I wasn't usually that kind of person, I preferred it when other people took control, and I was on the edge of things. I'd always felt safer that way, more secure. But now it was me who was having to be the rock, the stalwart anchor in the midst of this unthinkable horror.

'That's right,' Mum was saying in a soft voice. 'Let it all out, Ellen. You poor thing. I'm so sorry you had to witness such an awful sight.' She kept on stroking my hair, like she used to do when I was upset when I was little. 'You'll feel better eventually. Just give it time, my love.'

I'd spoken to her several times on the phone already that day; she'd seen some coverage about the incident on the news earlier and had immediately rung me to find out if I was all right, and if I'd heard about what happened, and how I felt. She said it was all the local news was focussing on, that it had become their main story. This knowledge just added to the feeling that everything had changed, been turned on its head, in seconds. The thought that I was caught up in a news story was so surreal I couldn't get my head around it. She said that Jack and I weren't featured on the news – thank God – that they were just showing shots of the outside of the Bryants' house, with news reporters talking urgently into cameras, telling the world the few facts about what had happened that the police had passed on to them.

I leaned away from her, wiping my eyes.

'But it's Jack who's hurt by this the most,' I managed, between gasps. 'Imagine what it was like for him, to find his beloved family strung up like that – all grey and dead. Oh God, Mum, it was so bloody horrendous. Seeing them all there, just hanging like that. Poor Sabrina. Poor Penelope. Poor all of them. I can't believe this has happened. How is Jack ever going to get past this? I'm so worried about him. He's in bits, he can't even speak. He can't cope.'

My mum listened to me ramble on, and then when my sobs had finally subsided she guided me into the kitchen, sat me down, and made me a very sweet, strong cup of tea.

'Here, drink that, love,' she said, placing the steaming mug on the table in front of me. She sat down on the chair next to me. 'Where's Jack now then? Is someone looking after him tonight?'

'He's with his aunt and uncle,' I said, placing my hands around the scalding-hot drink. The heat felt comforting. 'Marjorie and Patrick. They turned up and shouted at the house, trying to get Penelope to come outside. They were shouting so loudly. They had no idea what had happened, although the police seemed to want to question them about it.'

My mum gazed at me for a minute, then she sighed.

'Listen love,' she said. 'I know that you care about Jack a lot, and that you desperately want to help him right now. And I understand that, it shows what a lovely person you are. You've always been compassionate. I'll never forget how you looked after Granny's old cat that time she was sick, you wouldn't leave her side for one minute, bless you. But you need to be aware that the Bryant family is a complicated one.'

I stared at her, feeling the usual wave of irritation rise in me.

My mum was always saying derogatory things about Jack and his family, and it pissed me off. Of all days for her to start saying these things, today was not a good one. Not after everything that had happened; Christ, I'd seen Penelope, the grandmother, and most of the children hanging there in their conservatory, dead and awful-looking. My head was all over the place and I didn't want to hear anything that my mum had to say about them if it wasn't positive. Privately, I'd suspected for a while that my mum had always been a bit jealous of Penelope, who'd had the looks, money and husband – although she had been a widow – that I imagined my stoic mum might secretly want in her life. Since my dad left, she'd often seemed lonely, and I could only imagine what it had been like for her to see Penelope with her large brood of children swarming round her, in that big house. To see the expensive, quality furniture, the well-tended garden, the perfectly-dressed children. My mum's little garden looked like an overgrown area of wasteland. She kept saying that she was going to sort it out, but she never did. Mum had been brought up in Milton Keynes, in a boring estate called Westcroft where everything looked the same. She'd taken me back there once, and all the houses were made from identical red brick, and crammed tightly together. They were certainly very different from the opulent grand house that the Bryants owned.

'Can we just leave this topic for today?' I said, my tone suddenly sharp. I exhaled loudly.

'Don't get annoyed.' Mum made placating gestures with her hands. Her face looked so worn, so tired. I wished she'd take more time to take care of herself. 'I'm not being horrible about them or anything, Ellen. You really must understand that that's not my intention here. I just want you to be able to protect yourself. I think perhaps that I can see things that you can't, when it comes to the Bryants. All I'm trying to say is that things are not as perfect on the inside of that clan as they seem on the outside.'

'Yeah, well we all know that,' I said. 'I'm perfectly aware of the fact that Dalton wasn't very nice to Penelope some of the time. That all came out after he died, didn't it? But Jack says that his mum should have stood up to his dad more. He says that the problems they had were half her fault, and that she shouldn't have been such a doormat. He said that if she'd been stronger, then his dad would have backed down and not bullied her so much.'

I watched as an expression of something flitted across my mum's face. What was it, disbelief? Anger? I wasn't sure.

'Poor Penelope,' she said quietly, shaking her head. 'Yes, to think she was leading such a terrible existence for all those years. Dalton was a big bully, he made her life hell. No, that's not what I'm referring to here, Ellen.'

'What then?' I said. I was aware that I was coming across a bit snappy now, but I really couldn't see why she wasn't being fully supportive of Jack, given the horrific discovery he and I had just made. I mean, wasn't it obvious to her that he needed me more than ever now? Why couldn't we both be united in that thought for once?

Mum paused.

'I'm just trying to warn you about getting too involved in things that you don't fully understand,' she said. 'Not all families are transparent, love. Some have hidden agendas that you don't see until it's too late, and you've already become part of them. Just be careful, that's all.'

'What the hell are you talking about?' I said. I could feel my eyebrows lowering as I picked up the steaming mug and took a sip.

'I'm not exactly sure,' my mum said. 'I just get a feeling

about those Bryants, the whole extended lot of them. And especially after what's happened today...'

'Exactly,' I said, pushing my chair back and standing up. I picked up my tea. 'After what happened today, Jack needs me more than ever. And there's no way that I'm not going to support him as much as I can right now. He needs me, Mum. He's lost his whole immediate family. And just because his aunt and uncle are a bit weird and bossy, and you have a strange feeling about them, it doesn't mean I shouldn't be there for my best friend, does it?'

As I walked out of the kitchen, I heard my mum give a deep sigh.

'I've made up the bed in your old room for you,' she called.

'Thanks,' I said in a low voice, before heading up the stairs. If my mum thought she knew something that I didn't about the Bryants, then I wasn't interested in hearing it. Not today. Not after the horror of finding their bodies. Whatever she thought she knew probably wasn't true, anyway. Just local gossip from the busybodies that lived down her road who had nothing better to do than spread rumours about other people...

CHAPTER SIX

I awoke in the night, terrified, pulling at my neck, trying to loosen the noose that was wrapped tightly round it. As consciousness filtered slowly through my mind, I realised that it was all a dream. A fucking awful nightmare. It had been so vivid; I'd been made to stand on a stool by a shadowy, unidentified figure, who'd already hung the other members of my family. I remember looking around, and seeing my mum and Tom's faces, dead, their eyes open and staring blankly into space. My dad was there too, hanging separately to the rest of us. His face was mouldy green for some reason, and he'd died with a look of agony on his face that had become frozen in time. When the unseen person had tied the noose around my neck, the atmosphere in the nightmare became unbearable. I was pushed off the stool. The pain around my neck was beyond description, and I couldn't breathe. As my hands went to my neck, my feet thrashing around in mid-air, I realised that it wasn't just my family hanging from the roof in the room. The Bryants were there too, their faces dead and grey. *Oh my God, I can't believe I'm actually going to die like Sabrina did...*

That's when I'd woken up, sweating and shaking, gasping

for air. Realising I wasn't dying after all, that it had just been an awful dream. But I couldn't get back to sleep for ages after that. *I haven't really died, but Sabrina has*, I kept thinking. *Why her? Why her whole family? What did they do to deserve that? Could it really be suicide?* I just couldn't get my head round that concept. I mean, it was a stretch to imagine a double suicide – although I vaguely remember reading a story about one of those in Mum's newspaper a while ago. But six people choosing to end their lives together, all in one go? Now that was unheard of. Were there signs that they were all unhappy?

As I turned over in my bed yet again, trying to get comfortable, I had the horrible feeling that there probably had been signs. And that I'd chosen to ignore most of them, because I liked idolising the Bryants. I enjoyed looking up to them. And I'd wanted that feeling to go on and on. But there had been some things that I couldn't overlook; I'd never wanted to stare at those things too deeply, because I didn't want to shatter my image of my dream family. And I didn't want to look at them now either, I wanted to get back to sleep...

But as I flipped over again and again, willing a deep slumber to come, it didn't. The only thing my mind seemed to want to do was rake through my memories of Jack and his family, examining anything that might have seemed off, or wrong, in the past. I closed my eyes tight, willing all my worries to go away. But they didn't. Despite my best efforts, my eyes opened again...

CHAPTER SEVEN

E arly the next morning, the ringing of my phone jolted me out of a deep sleep.

'Er, hello?' I said, answering it with my eyes half shut.

'Ellen?' It was Jack. 'I'm at the flat. Where are you?'

As soon as I heard his voice, all remnants of sleep fell away from me.

'I'm at my mum's,' I said. 'I didn't want to be on my own there last night. Your aunt told me that you'd be staying with them. I hope you had at least some sleep last night, Jack, you really needed it. Anyway, how are you?' He sounded a lot better than he had yesterday. More chipper and energised. And he was talking in full sentences, which was a huge improvement on the day before.

'Very sad,' Jack said. 'I can't believe that this has happened to my family. I miss you, Ellen. I really need to be with you right now. When will you be coming back here?'

I was already pushing off my duvet and swinging my legs over the side of the bed.

'I'll be there soon,' I said, rifling through yesterday's clothes that were in a bunch on the chair. Although I'd moved out to my own flat now, loads of my possessions were still at my mum's, including – thank God – some underwear. 'I'll be there in about half an hour. Just stay at the flat, Jack, and I'll be with you very soon, okay?'

'All right,' he said. 'Don't be too long.'

Despite the horror that had happened, I couldn't help my stomach from doing a little leap. Jack needed me. He missed me. He'd said these things himself. I flung my phone on the bed, dressed quickly, slapped a bit of lipstick on, put my phone into my handbag and made my way downstairs. I would never, ever tell Jack how I really felt about him, that I'd been in love with him for quite a while – this was something I'd only just been able to admit to myself, because we were best friends, and I didn't want to do anything that spoiled the closeness between us. And to be honest, I didn't think he had the same feelings for me. Although sometimes he said things that made me wonder...

'Morning, love.' My mum looked up from her paper. 'Did you sleep okay?'

'Yep.' I smiled at her as I poured myself some fresh orange juice. 'I've got to go out now, Mum.'

She glanced up at the clock. I followed her gaze. It had just gone nine in the morning.

'That's a shame,' she said. 'I was hoping you'd stay here and have a good rest today. You looked so tired yesterday evening.'

'I just have to meet someone,' I said. 'I'll probably stay at my flat tonight, but I'll come and see you again very soon, okay? Also, Nala will be absolutely starving by now, and I need to go and feed her.' I wasn't going to tell her it was Jack, as I didn't want to listen to another one of her sermons about how complicated his family was.

Mum smiled, but her eyes looked sad for some reason. Mind you, they nearly always did these days. Her depression had made her look even older than she was, and I didn't like it. I wanted so much for her to be happy, and to find her zest for life again.

'Okay, love,' she said. 'I'm always here if you need me, just remember that, all right?'

'Thanks,' I said, as I turned and made my way towards the front door.

As I passed one of the neighbour's houses, I saw the daily newspaper – *The Buckingham Echo* – balanced on their stone wall.

Six Family Members Found Hanging, I read. There was a large photo of the Bryants' house. *Six members of the same family were found hanging in their conservatory yesterday, a police officer confirmed to the Echo. One is believed to be Penelope Bryant, an upstanding member of the Buckingham community, who has been very active in her local church over recent years. 'I can't believe this has happened,' a neighbour said. 'It's so safe round here. At least, it used to be.' Police are remaining tight-lipped about the causes of death, and Detective Sergeant Moretti, who is now leading the investigation, said that he has no further information he could pass on to us at this time.*

Shit, I thought, walking on. Tears started rolling down my cheeks, and I brushed them away, annoyed. I couldn't afford to lose it now, I had to be strong for Jack. As I carried on down Mum's road and rounded the corner towards Buckingham town, my phone rang again. Jack's name was flashing. I answered it.

'I'm nearly there,' I said. 'Just give me five minutes.'

'That detective, DS Moretti just phoned me.' Jack's voice sounded loud, and his words were tumbling out quickly. 'I can't cope with this, Ellen. I don't know how I'm going to keep going, I'm not sure that I can, it's all just too hard to bear...'

CHAPTER EIGHT

As I ran, memories of the younger Jack began flashing through my mind. Jack teasing the neighbour's cat in the garden, twelve-year-old Jack looking all lanky in his school uniform, big brother Jack giving Sabrina a hug when she was crying. It had always baffled me that Jack, Sabrina and the rest of their siblings got on with each other so well. When Tom was living at home, we'd had what Mum said was a normal sibling relationship; meaning we tried to kill each other half the time. I mean, there were lots of instances when we actually got on, but most of the time he was just really bloody annoying and wound me up as much as he could. He came into my room to fart, he hit me when I wouldn't give him the TV remote, he told tales to Mum about me when we were little. He said that I was bossy and controlling towards him, which may or may not be true; I just tried to organise him into being less of a twat. On the rare occasions that I went to another child's party, from what I could see, most of the people in my class had similar relationships with their siblings to mine. But the Bryant children weren't like that. They seemed to be more mature in their dealings with each other, and the younger ones even admired the older ones. I was quite certain that Tom would never admire me if I was the last person left in the universe. I just didn't understand the dynamics in the Bryant household; but I wanted to so badly. The whole lot of them fascinated me. And Jack, being the eldest, was the one they – and I – looked up to the most.

Oh poor Jack, I thought, willing my legs to pump faster. *He just doesn't deserve this. How on earth is he going to get past it? God, I hope he's going to be okay...*

CHAPTER NINE

I was out of breath as I arrived at the communal door of my flat, and at first I couldn't get the key into the lock as my hand was shaking too much. After several attempts, and internally telling myself to calm down, I managed it, and a few seconds later I was opening my own door and walking into my little two-bed apartment, and found Jack pacing back and forth across the living-room floor, raking his hands through his hair.

I'd started running as soon as Jack had said the words, 'It's all just too hard to bear,' and all I could think was that my friend was about to do something stupid to himself because of the pain he was in. All I'd known is that I had to get to him as soon as possible, because I knew that anyone who'd gone through what Jack had yesterday would be on a knife edge mentally right now, and Jack had sounded so desperate when he'd phoned...

'Hey, Jack?' I said, my voice hoarse, walking towards him. 'Are you okay?'

He turned to me, and I had to stop the shock showing on my face. My beautiful Jack, who always looked so suave and together, was a wreck of a man. Of course, this was to be expected, he mustn't have slept a wink the night before; I mean, how could anyone sleep when they were wondering why on earth their whole family were found dead, and trussed up like Christmas turkeys? When they realised that all of their immediate relatives had been annihilated in one fell swoop? His eyes were hollow and grey, his skin pallid, his hair a mess. He had stains on his shirt, and it looked like he'd slept in his clothes. Nala was winding in and out of his legs, meowing loudly, clearly hungry.

'No, not really,' Jack said.

I stepped forwards and gave him a tight hug, loving feeling the warmth of his body in my arms. I knew I shouldn't, but I really enjoyed that moment. I loved how he smelled, how he felt, everything. I wished that I could do this all the time...

'What happened with the detective?' I said, when I finally released him from my grip.

Jack sighed.

'Just that the autopsies will take place today,' he said. 'And that they are still unsure whether the cause of everyone's deaths was suicide or murder, but that they're doing all they can. We'll just have to try and be patient, and see what they find out.'

'Oh Jack,' I said. 'I'm so, so sorry that this has happened to you. It's too awful.'

'Thanks Ellen,' he said, reaching out to give my hand a squeeze. 'You've always been such a good friend to me. You've always been there when I've needed someone. I'm so lucky to have you in my life.' My heart did a flip, despite the horror of the situation. *I'm so lucky to have you in my life*, Jack had just said. *Well*, I thought. *If one good thing comes out of all of this, it might be that Jack and I get even closer. I think we're good for each other. And then maybe one day, who knows what might happen...*

'DS Moretti said that he can't really tell me any more than that at the moment,' Jack went on. 'He said that him and his officers are working on the case as hard as they can, and that

A PERFECT FAMILY

he'll let me know as soon as they have more news. He said that none of them are going to rest until they've discovered how and why my family ended up hanging like that in the conservatory. He said he is going to need me to come in and have a chat with him very soon, because he couldn't talk to me yesterday when I was having a breakdown. What did you say to them, by the way? I was with it enough to notice the detective calling you out of the room at one point.'

'Oh, I just explained that we'd been together all of Friday, as it was my birthday,' I said. 'That we'd spent the day and lots of the evening and night watching films and eating and drinking, and that I knew you'd been there all night as when I woke up you were snoring in your bed. I even showed them the photos of us that I'd posted on Facebook, Jack. I was as honest as I could be, as I just want to help them find out what the hell happened here.'

Jack nodded. He looked so forlorn.

'Oh God,' I said, sinking down on to the sofa, with Nala immediately jumping on to my knee and meowing loudly at me. 'How are you feeling, Jack? This must all be so awful for you.'

Jack looked at me, and gave me a twisted smile.

'I feel like I'm on an escalator to hell,' he said. 'It's all a fucking nightmare, Ellen. Like I said on the phone, I have no idea how I'm going to get through all this. But I'm glad you're here. Do you know what I need to do right now?'

'What?' I said.

'I need to get really drunk,' Jack said. 'And you need to come with me and get hammered, too.'

33

CHAPTER TEN

I only hesitated for a second. Something that my mum had said a few weeks ago went round in my head: 'You always seem to follow Jack, Ellen. He clicks his fingers, and you come running. I just hope that he's there for you in the same way, when you need a supportive friend.' Her words had annoyed me at the time, and they pissed me off now that I was thinking about them. I was my own person, I could say no if I didn't want to do something, I didn't follow Jack round like a sheep or anything. Well, not really. It wasn't like I was completely under his spell or anything. But now, the truth was that I could see the logic in what he wanted to do. A bit of alcohol would probably dull the emotional pain he was in. Be a type of anaesthetic for his grief and shock. It might help mine too, I mean, my head had been completely fucked up by finding the poor bodies hanging there. So maybe it wasn't such a bad idea...

'Okay,' I said, standing up again. 'Just give me five minutes so I can feed the cat, she'll bite my arm off in a minute. Which pub do you want to go to?'

Twenty minutes later, we were both ensconced in a booth in The Bull and Butcher pub, me with a pint of Amstel in front of me, and Jack with the remnants of a double whisky and Coke in his hands. We knew the place well, as we often went there for a drink or two. There are loads of pubs in and around Buckingham, partly because it's a university town, and partly because most of the residents like a social drink. The Bull and Butcher has always been one of my favourites, because of the relaxed atmosphere in it, and because of its old beams and fireplace; I always feel really cosy whenever I'm there. I didn't get that feeling today though. I still had icy chills in me because of yesterday's horror, and I kept looking over at Jack, hoping that he wasn't about to get so drunk that he made himself ill. I'd never tell him what to do though, I wouldn't want him to think that I was a hen-pecking type of person. I was just glad that he wanted to be with me today, and I knew for sure that I was going to make every effort to be there for him, because I loved him, and he'd been through such an awful time. And from what he'd said back at my flat, Jack seemed to really value spending time with me, too...

When we'd first walked in, the fat old man behind the bar – Joel the landlord – had looked surprised. He knew us to chat to, as we'd been in there so many times before, even when I was underage. I wouldn't have gone drinking with anyone other than Jack when I was seventeen. He was a nice guy, and always made his regulars feel at home. He'd lived in Buckingham all his life, and seemed to know everything about everyone. He was like a local treasure, a friend to the masses.

'Hello mate,' he'd said to Jack. 'Listen, I'm so sorry to hear about what happened to your family. It's beyond awful. I guess I didn't expect you to be out and about so soon, but they say everyone responds to grief differently, eh?'

News spread fast in a close community, plus I knew from my mum that the media had been reporting on it since shortly after we'd found their bodies. She said most of the shots shown on the TV were of the outside of the Bryants' house, which was now surrounded by police tape. I'd been expecting most people to know, but still, it was weird hearing Joel's sympathy. It made the whole situation more real. Like it had actually happened. Which it had. Shit, I needed a lager so badly.

'I just need a drink please, Joel,' Jack had said in his cut-glass accent. He told him what we both wanted.

Nodding, with understanding floating across his face, Joel had turned and got our drinks ready without another word. A few other people had come over to give Jack their condolences, their body language awkward, and their speech hesitant, stuttering. I mean, how do you acknowledge something so dreadful to the only surviving family member of such a horrendous situation? Most of the people looked relieved when their words were out and they could turn away and go back to their tables and their calmer, more ordinary non-traumatised lives.

A group of girls that I didn't like, who went to Buckingham University but were thankfully on a different course to me, were sitting in the corner; the arch-bitch Layla in the middle of them. She'd been in my class at school, she was always one of the 'popular' girls, but God knows why, as I'd noticed that she had a habit of being nice to people's faces, then slagging them off behind their backs. She was quite pretty in a brassy kind of way, although I personally thought that she always wore too much make-up. She'd been friends with Jack's sister Sabrina too, not like I was, they'd been more superficial mates who would invite each other to their birthday parties and things but not speak for the rest of the year. Layla had never made any secret about the fact that she fancied Jack. She'd never exactly been subtle about it, everyone knew how she felt. But then loads of girls loved him; it wasn't hard to see why, he was a gorgeous specimen of a human being. But he never seemed to notice the swooning females around him; he'd only ever had one serious girlfriend to my knowledge – Holly – but that had ended about a year ago when Holly and her family moved out of the area. I'd had my suspicions that there was something going on between him and Layla at one point, particularly when Layla walked past me slowly one day with the smuggest smirk plastered on her face. But Jack never said anything about it, and in the end I presumed that I'd imagined it. I had admitted the depths of my feelings for Jack to myself now, and although it was hard as he didn't seem to reciprocate the love very much, it was a relief to acknowledge that it was there, burning away in me from the moment I woke up, to the point that I dropped off to sleep. Just spending time with him would have to do me, and I was happy enough with that. I had to be okay with it.

Soon it was just me and Jack sitting in a corner booth alone.

'I'm going to get another drink,' Jack said, staring at his now empty glass. 'Do you want me to line you up another pint, Ellen, or are you still going with that one?'

'Er, I'm fine at the moment, thanks,' I said, picking up my glass. I've never been a big drinker, and I usually stick to lager. But I can't drink it fast because it makes me feel sick if I do.

Minutes later, Jack returned to the table holding three glasses. They all looked like double whisky and Cokes.

'Thought I'd get a few in now.' He gave me a look. 'Saves me going back and forth to the bar, you know?'

I nodded and tried to smile, but I was feeling nervous now. He was obviously on a mission.

We drank in silence for a while.

'Ellen, listen,' he said, turning to me as he drained away the second of his new drinks. He picked up the third glass. 'There's something I need to get off my chest, I've been wanting to talk to someone about it for ages, but I've never felt free enough to say anything before.'

I stared at him. What was he going to say? That he liked me, in a way that was stronger than platonic friendship? Strange time to bring it up, but I wasn't going to argue. I held my breath, and nodded.

'Now that my family is dead I can tell you,' he said. 'Something bad was going on in my house, before my dad died. I think what he did really fucked my head up, Ellen. It's so weird. I'm going to tell you something that I've never told anyone before. I have to, I have to get the words out. I really hope you understand what I'm about to say, you're always so kind to me...'

CHAPTER ELEVEN

A reel of thoughts flashed through my mind in an instant. *Oh God*, I was thinking. *Please don't tell me bad things about your family, Jack...* Even though we'd found his family members grey and dead, my idolisation of his family had become so important in my life that I didn't know if I could take having my image of them destroyed. It was like, even though she was now dead, I still kind of aspired to be like Sabrina, I wanted to emulate her self-possessed confidence so badly. It would be my tribute to her, to carry on her legacy throughout my life. Normally, I could never quite manage it, but that was my aim. But if Jack was about to tell me awful things about what went on in his home, then everything I had believed about the Bryants over the years would fall into question. My ideal family would be more broken than they already were, and I didn't know if I was ready for that. I wanted to keep the past – as I saw it – untarnished.

But as I looked into Jack's sad eyes, my heart lurched and I realised that I couldn't be selfish about that anymore. That if my friend, my beloved Jack, had secrets that he wanted to get off his chest, it was my duty to shut up and listen, and put his wellbeing before mine. If he had unsavoury truths to tell me, then I just had to take them. And if that meant that my fantasies were destroyed, then so be it...

CHAPTER TWELVE

I sat and listened to Jack talk, a horrible numbness taking me over. I drank my pint much more quickly than I normally would.

'My dad,' Jack was saying. 'The wonderful Dalton Bryant who everyone seemed to revere, was actually a monster, Ellen. Yes, I know you know all about how rude he was to my mother; that's no secret – not after her friend started gossiping once Dad was dead and buried. But things went on in our house that no one has any idea about. Terrible, awful things, that you never had any idea about.'

'Like what?' I managed, not sure I actually wanted to hear his reply.

'Dad was more than strict,' Jack said. 'He wasn't just an old-fashioned authoritarian. He could be evil sometimes. Power over us went to his head, especially after we'd moved back to Buckingham and started growing up. He couldn't handle watching me and Sabrina becoming more independent, and understanding more about human nature and the world. He did some really terrible things to try and keep us under his control.'

I nodded, wishing I could go and get another pint now, but

not wanting to be rude and leave when he was telling me such an important thing.

'He knew we'd never tell anyone about what he was doing while he was alive,' Jack went on. 'We were all too scared of him. Even now, I've had to get a few drinks into me before I can tell you about it. I don't think I'll ever get over how he treated us.'

'What did he do?' I asked.

Jack paused, then took a big swig of his remaining drink.

'The worst bit started when Dad convinced himself that what we were learning at church wasn't enough,' he said. 'That it wasn't giving us a strong enough message to stay on the right path. He saw us growing up, particularly me and Sabrina, and I think it frightened him, because he could see that one day we would be old enough to properly think for ourselves, and that we might leave him. That we might become able to question his rule, and move away from it. So he started holding extra religious meetings at home. We all had to attend, my mum, my sisters and my brother. Even Granny had to come, when she moved in with us after Grandad died. Dad got really bad at that point, when Granny came to stay. I've never understood why.'

I nodded, wondering what the hell Jack was going to say next. I realised that I was holding my breath.

'Dad would say that God was speaking to us through him,' Jack said, shaking his head a little. 'That we needed to do exactly what he said, because if we didn't, we would be offending God. And to offend God is the highest sin.'

I stared at my friend. I knew that Jack's parents were very religious, I mean, even my mum had taken me to church when I was little – until Dad had that affair with the lady who ironed Father Achebe's robes. After that we only went at Christmas and Easter. I knew the Bryants were much more devout than we'd ever been, and occasionally Sabrina or Jack would make a religious reference that surprised me. But there's no way that I'd ever thought that religion dominated their lives to this extent, or that Dalton had been some sort of religious maniac. After he'd died and I'd found out how horrible he'd been to Penelope, my opinion of him had changed. But none of his children had ever given a sign that anything else – other than him being dominating – had been going on behind closed doors. I mean, Sabrina had told me about how stubborn and controlling her dad could be when she opened up to me that day. But she'd said nothing about any of this. Could people really mask a secret to this extent? Even to their friends?

'I believe that he was speaking the truth when he said that,' Jack went on. I blinked.

'What do you mean?' I said.

'I mean, I believe that offending God is the highest sin that there is,' Jack said. 'Don't you, Ellen?'

'Um,' I said. 'To be honest, I'm not really sure what I think about religion, Jack. I mean, there's so much corruption in it, isn't there?'

'Yes, but that's human corruption.' Jack turned to me, and I saw that his eyes were gleaming. 'If there's anything wrong with the way churches are run on this Earth, then that's because the humans involved have failed God. But God himself can't be corrupted. Don't you see? He's the infinite, infallible source of power over the world. His word is law. And to offend him is to book yourself a certain place in hell.'

'Okay,' I said slowly. I'd never heard Jack talk like this before, and it was really unsettling me. But then I'd never seen him drink four whisky and Cokes so quickly either. He's probably a bit drunk, I decided. He's probably rambling. He'll think differently about all this tomorrow. He'll have chilled out by then, and will have stopped raving like a maniac. 'But what did your dad do that was so upsetting?'

Jack paused, then sighed.

'He always made out that none of us were doing well enough for God,' he said. 'Dad monitored all of us all the time, and kept saying that we weren't helping enough around the house, or listening to him properly, or that we should pray more. That we weren't atoning properly for our mistakes, and that unless we made ourselves useful from morning to night, we were letting God – and him – down. He said that he'd never been as lazy or insolent as us when he was young. It got to the point where he bought himself a notebook, and started writing down the messages that God was giving to us, through him.'

My mouth opened. Dalton was now sounding like a crazy person, if what Jack was saying was true. I was finding his words hard to listen to, and I no longer knew what to think or believe. But as I gazed at Jack's long lashes, and the pained expression on his face, something told me to keep my doubts to myself. I was there to support my friend, and he would be so hurt if he thought that I didn't believe what he was saying. It wasn't the time to enter into some sort of theological debate.

'Christ, Jack,' I said. 'You poor thing. Why didn't you or Sabrina say something to me about this at the time?'

'We couldn't.' Jack raised his eyebrows. 'Don't you see, Ellen? Dad had all of us under such control. We knew that if we ever spoke out about anything he did, he would punish us so severely that our lives wouldn't be worth living. And his behaviour was already bad enough. He locked us in the cellar and whipped us when he was feeling particularly annoyed. And I kind of agreed with lots of the things that he said – his teachings about God. It was, and is, so hard to separate the things that I think he was wrong about, with the things I think he got right. I don't know if you can understand that?'

'Yes.' I nodded slowly. 'I do get what you mean.'

'By the time he died,' Jack said, 'Dad was writing down

daily instructions for all of us in his notebooks – that he said were messages from God. He would write criticisms, too, and tell all of us to monitor each other, and to admonish anyone who was stepping out of line and not doing as they were told. Even after he'd died, the atmosphere in the house was still awful. He'd done the damage by then, you see, and we all felt broken. I couldn't wait to move out. One day I just woke up and realised that I'd had enough of living there, and that I needed a fresh start, and to be someplace where I could heal and find myself again. That's when I asked you if it would be okay if I moved in to your spare room. You were such a love for letting me. I'd never felt so free as I did the day that I moved in with you. I know this sounds bad, but I was kind of glad when Dad died. Isn't that awful?' His face creased up, pain washing through it.

'No,' I said, meaning it. 'No, Jack, it's not awful, it's completely understandable. The way Dalton was making you all live at home was extremely wrong. It was abusive. You poor things. No wonder your mum started looking even more exhausted than usual. No one deserves to live under those conditions, and he should have never made all your lives such a living hell. Poor Penelope.'

'Yeah,' a snarl came into Jack's voice, 'but she failed as a parent too, didn't she? I mean, Mum could see what Dad was doing to all of us, but she never stepped in to protect us or anything. She just went along with whatever he instructed her to do. It was like she was his puppet. She was broken inside. It was pathetic to see her so house-trained. It was like she was his robot.'

I was shocked at this, and I had to bite my tongue. The way he spoke about his mum upset me. Yes, Penelope probably never had stood up for herself in the face of her dominating husband. And I could see why Jack felt let down by this. But his mum had always been so sweet to me, she just always seemed like such an easy person to love. She was naturally so kind. I didn't understand my friend's animosity towards her, especially as she was now lying cold in a morgue. I looked over and saw that Jack's glass was empty now, and that he was eying up the bar again, no doubt planning his next drink.

'Let me get some more drinks in,' I said quickly. I suddenly felt like I needed a breather from this intense conversation. 'Same again?'

Jack nodded.

As I walked over to the bar, my mum's words came back to me. 'The Bryant family is a complicated one', she'd said. Did my own mother know more about them than she'd let on? I wondered. But if so, why had she never told me more details? I had a feeling that I would have to go and see her again soon, and ask her to tell me what it was that she knew...

CHAPTER THIRTEEN

The next hour or so became a blur. Jack sometimes happy, sometimes sad. Him bringing back multiple drinks from the bar, sometimes with a bag of crisps in tow. I knew he'd always liked to drink, he said it helped him write. I'd never been allowed to read any of his stories – he always joked that I'd be the first person to receive a copy of his book when it came out in print. He'd told me before that when he drank wine, as he sat in front of his laptop, he could feel his brain relaxing, and imaginative thoughts start to pour through. I'd asked about his subject matter many times, but Jack was always rather coy about that.

'Crime,' he'd say. 'I've researched it, and it's the most popular genre.'

'True crime?' I'd enquire.

'No, not all of it,' he'd reply with a smile. 'Now stop asking questions, Ellen. You know I can't write anything if I tell people what I'm doing. It stops the creative process from flowing if I give too much away.'

I tried not to worry about the fact that there never seemed to be any results from all Jack's writing. *But books must take time to compose,* I always told myself. *Just be patient, Ellen. He'll probably surprise you one day, by telling you that he's got the most amazing publishing deal.*

As I gazed at my friend waltzing round the pub with his umpteenth whisky and Coke in his hand, I reflected, for the thousandth time, what a bright spark Jack could be when he was in the right mood. How he could connect with other people so easily. I knew it was strange, that he was becoming so animated the day after his family had died. But I had no doubt that this was his way of coping with his grief; by getting pissed out of his brain. And who was I to say that this was a bad thing?

CHAPTER FOURTEEN

By lunchtime, I was steaming drunk. In the end, it had seemed easier to join Jack in his mission to enter alcoholic oblivion than to try to give him a pep talk about sobering up, and to be honest, after what he'd told me about Dalton's messages from God, I was ready to dull my overloaded mind. I now realised that what I'd believed – that they were such a perfect family – was a load of bullshit. *Why hadn't I seen the truth?* I wondered. I knew why, it had been because I hadn't wanted to believe anything bad about them, and because they'd kept most of it hidden. They were like actors in a play, all pretending to be someone else. Hiding their truths. Jack was in a huge amount of pain, but now so was I. Sabrina had been my friend, and although the situation was much worse for him, it was still pretty horrific for me. The thought of encountering a dead body had always scared me, and I'd never seen one until yesterday. And then I'd seen six in one go. When Jack suggested that we drink some Jägerbombs, I was already pissed enough to readily agree. I was enjoying the thick numbing sensation that was flooding my brain.

I'm not going to lie, I can't remember much after I'd had my second. I can remember vague flashes of things, like Jack shouting at someone, Joel the landlord asking us to leave, Jack pissing up against a fence in broad daylight, us getting hold of more alcohol from some shop, and then ending up back at my flat. We drank more, and I honestly don't remember who did what or how it came about, but all I know is that I woke up in a dark room hours later, completely naked, lying on my bed next to Jack who – from what I could feel – also had nothing on. From the way he was snoring, I knew he was still passed out, which wasn't surprising as he'd drunk even more than me.

My head was pounding as I leaned sideways very slowly, and looked at the glowing digits on my alarm clock. It was nearly 10pm. Fuck, the whole day had disappeared in an unexpected oblivion of drunkenness. I switched my bedside light on. Nala was curled up at the bottom of the duvet. Jack's eyelids didn't even flicker, he was clearly out for the count. By the looks of things – i.e. the used condom on the floor – Jack and I had slept together. Damn it, I'd been wanting this to happen for so long, and now that it had I couldn't even remember doing it. Oh well, hopefully it would happen again, sooner rather than later...

I got up very slowly, and went into the bathroom. I turned the shower on, and just stood still under the warm, flowing water for ages. Eventually, I managed to summon up the energy to wash myself properly. I was mentally kicking myself all the time, for not being able to remember having sex with Jack. I mean, seriously? Something had happened that I'd been desperate for for so long, and I couldn't even remember it? Just my bloody luck. I'd only ever had one boyfriend before, Freddie, and he had been a bit weird and into trains. And our relationship had only lasted a month. It hadn't exactly been a fulfilling time. Jack was in a completely different class to him. Also, I felt sick and my head was still thumping. Having a hangover in the evening felt weird, but the soothing water did help me to feel a bit brighter.

When I was dry and dressed in some clean clothes, I brushed my soaking hair then made my way into the kitchen. After downing two paracetamol with a glass of water, I opened the fridge and stared at the uninspiring items inside it. A small bit of cheese, the end of a pint of milk, half a red pepper and some butter. Wow. I reckoned I was going to have to order a pizza, as an insatiable hunger had just taken me over, and if I had enough cash in my purse then a takeaway was definitely the only way to go. I grabbed my bag, got my purse out and had a look, and was relived to find a crumpled twenty pound note stuffed in one of the pockets.

It didn't take long to order an extra-large meat feast from the local pizza place. The man on the phone told me it would be with me in about half an hour, which at that point seemed like an eternity away. So to distract myself from my aching belly, I began to tidy up the mess that we'd obviously made when we'd come back from the pub – the one I barely had any recollection of making. I was now a bit annoyed at myself for getting so drunk, as it wasn't usually something I liked to do. I enjoyed a social drink with friends – not that I really saw Kim or Jane much anymore, as Jack didn't seem to like them much so I'd stopped inviting them to the flat – but I hated having that out-of-control feeling of not remembering exactly what I'd said or done for a few hours. I'd only got that bladdered once before, at Jane's eighteenth birthday party. And the next day I'd vowed that I'd never get into that state again. That had been just over six months ago. And I'd kept that promise to myself. Until today...

I collected up the empty whisky bottle, the crumpled lager and cider cans, and the bottle of red wine that had clearly been knocked off the coffee table at some point and had leaked all over the carpet. Why had I drunk this much? I mean, yes, I was in a lot of pain. And I wanted to support my beloved Jack as much as I could, and he'd been on a complete mission to get as drunk as possible, for understandable reasons. He had a lot to block out. But I should have been a better friend, I should have been more responsible and somehow got him out of the pub earlier. This was a mess, and I now felt like shit. And I couldn't even remember us having sex, which was something I'd fantasised about for so long. Damn it.

My mood now low, I crushed the bottles and cans into the recycling bin in the kitchen, then returned to the living room and started picking up Jack's possessions that had somehow been strewn around the room. As I lifted up his jacket, something fell out of one of the pockets. I bent down to pick it up. It was a very old, worn sheet of paper, folded, with biro scribbles all over it. It looked like it had been torn out of an old notebook. Surely this couldn't be some of Dalton's rantings that Jack had been telling me about earlier?

CHAPTER FIFTEEN

I stood up, and looked towards the hall. Jack was still fast asleep, and by the sound of him he wouldn't wake up for hours. I knew that I shouldn't poke my nose into his business, but I wanted to help him so much, and if I read what was on the paper then it might help me do this in some way. That was how I rationalised my snooping to myself, as I opened up the page and began to read. It was dated just over four years ago, which would have been just before Dalton's death.

Sabrina has not been behaving well at all this week, the small, tight writing said. *The Lord is displeased, and commands you all to make sure that she does not have access to her phone from the minute she comes back from school. He is worried that by talking to her friends on social media, she is distracting herself from more important things like prayer, family and study. God has given me the knowledge that Jack is turning out just like my insolent brother, Jacob. He says he is too strong-minded and independent, and must be brought to heel at all costs, otherwise he will fall out permanently with his family and the Lord will not be able to save him. Adele has been doing better this week, and must make sure she continues to follow her father's rules. Zara needs constant monitoring, as she is eating too much and has put on more weight. Greed is a sin, and must be stopped before it gets out of hand. Samuel is the most dutiful at the moment. God says that Penelope is not performing her household tasks with due efficiency, and must be berated if anyone sees her slacking...*

I lowered my hands. I couldn't bear to read any more. Poor Jack. Poor everyone. Dalton had been a tyrant; I literally couldn't believe that anyone had the gall to talk to their family members like this. It was unreal. How had they all put up with it for so long? And they'd actually taken the bullshit that he'd written down seriously? *I guess that's the power of brainwashing,* I thought. Which was weird, as it was something I'd heard about but had never experienced happening first hand. I folded the sheet back up again, stuffed it into one of the pockets in Jack's coat, and then hung the coat up on one of the pegs by the front door.

As I turned to walk back into the living room, the doorbell rang, making me jump. Shit, I was a bag of nerves at the moment. I looked through the spyhole, and saw a young guy on the other side of the door, holding a pizza box. Of course, I'd ordered some food. It had arrived much quicker than I'd thought it was going to. Good, I was starving.

Ten minutes later, I'd devoured half of the pizza, enjoying every cheesy, delicious bite of it, every greasy morsel of meat. At that point, I'd forced myself to close the box and save the rest for Jack, even though I could quite happily have eaten the rest of it. But he deserved to have some food too. A noise behind me made me look up. My best friend was wandering into the room, looking very bleary eyed. He was wearing my dressing gown.

'Hi,' I said. 'How are you feeling?'

'Water,' he said, his voice sounding dry. 'I need water.'

I watched as he made his way towards the sink.

Five minutes later, we were sitting together on the sofa. Jack was already on his second slice of pizza. I was having an internal struggle, wondering whether to admit to seeing the piece of paper that had fallen out of his pocket.

'So,' he said, turning towards me and raising his eyebrows. 'I guess we...' He stopped and gave a small grin.

'Er, we must have done,' I said, annoyed at the hot blush I could feel spreading throughout my cheeks. 'Although I have to be honest, Jack, I can't remember much after we arrived back here and carried on drinking.'

'Phew, neither can I,' Jack said. I stared at him, thinking how gorgeous he looked with his hair all tousled and messy. God, I loved this man so much, and he had no idea how strong my feelings were for him. It just didn't feel right to tell him about how I felt, and I knew he wasn't the emotional sort who would divulge his feelings for me back – if he had any, which I didn't think he did. Not in that way. I was pretty sure that Jack thought of me as his best friend, and that was about it. I was just happy to be near him, it was as though I could feel some sort of magnetic force drawing me to him. To be honest, I'd felt like this for years, although the feeling had got noticeably stronger over time. I think that's why I hadn't been so close with Sabrina for a while. Although we never spoke about it directly, I could tell from the way I caught her looking at me sometimes that she knew I had feelings for her brother. And I know she was annoyed that I would sometimes spend more time with him than with her. It must have been weird for her, seeing this change in me. But I couldn't help it, it was as though this feeling of love for him had totally taken me over. I was helpless to it, I couldn't fight against it. I could even see that Jack had flaws – he could be arrogant sometimes, and a bit lazy – but I didn't care. I just wanted to be near him, because when I was, I felt lit up in a way that was so addictively wonderful, I just needed it to keep going on and on. When he'd asked to move in to my spare room, my heart had literally backflipped for a week, even though at the time, I'd try to play it cool and not let my excitement show too much.

Jack's lighter mood began to lower again, as he finished off the last slice and closed the lid of the pizza box. Nala wandered in, sat on the floor, and started washing herself. She always seemed to love being with people, much preferring to be near us than to be curled up in a room by herself.

'You know, Ellen,' he said. 'The police reckon they don't know whether the deaths of Granny, Mum, Sabrina, Sam, Adele and Zara were caused by suicide or murder. But deep down, I know the truth.'

The hairs on the back of my neck stood up. What on earth was he going to say now?

'What do you know?' I said.

'It was suicide.' Jack exhaled heavily as he said this. 'It must have been. Look, I remember a lot of this morning, before we came back here and got absolutely trollied. I know that I told you about Dad's notebooks, and how he would tell us that God was constantly criticising us for not doing well enough. Well, one day, he wrote a page saying that God was getting tired of our faults, and that if we couldn't rectify them soon, he would call us all home to him. The implication was definitely on God directing us all to take our own lives, if we didn't pull our socks up.' He stopped, and shook his head. 'They must have got to the stage where – for some reason – they decided to take his words about this seriously. I mean, how else do you get six people to hang themselves? It would be impossible, even for the most experienced serial killer in the world.'

I nodded.

'It's so awful, what your dad did, Jack,' I said, feeling tears spring into my eyes. I was devastated that my best friend and his siblings, mother and granny had had to endure this kind of abuse for so long in silence. And that Dalton might have potentially brainwashed them all into thinking that taking their lives was the right thing to do. And to me, that's exactly what it was: abuse. I didn't want to get into that with Jack right now, in case he started going on about religion and God's word again. I didn't think I could take that right now. But it seemed that he and his family had been groomed by Dalton into thinking that they should really believe that these messages were from God. That perhaps they were being called 'home'. It was insane. 'Yes, maybe you're right. Maybe they did all commit suicide for that reason. But the police still have to investigate all possibilities, in case something else caused them all to die like that. It's important that the actual truth comes out, isn't it?'

Jack looked at me, then nodded slowly.

'Yeah,' he said. 'You're right. But I bet you anything that the autopsy report will come back with that verdict.'

Maybe, I thought, it would be best if it did turn out to be suicide. Because that would mean that there wasn't a mass murderer walking around in Buckingham scot-free. And that was a thought that had been slowly creeping up on me, since we found the six bodies. If his family had been murdered, then why? I wasn't quite as ready as Jack to believe in only the suicide theory. I mean, he had been brainwashed by Dalton for years, and so he knew how powerful these messages from 'God' could be, and the impact that they could have on people. But thinking back – although I didn't want to – to the way the bodies had been strung up from the conservatory roof, there was something just not right about the whole thing. It was weird; wrong. Why would Adele, Zara and Samuel want to take their own lives? They were so young. Even if they had been coerced into it, it was still wrong. I could feel that my mind was trying to tell me something about the scene, trying to flag up something I was missing. And then the realisation came to me, and smacked me between the eyes. There had been two fans whirring away in the conservatory. When I'd moved to let one of the paramedics past, I'd nearly fallen over a stool, and had knocked it into one of the fans, which wobbled. At the time, none of this had registered as important. But now, as I cast my mind back, two things about this struck me as odd. The big pile of notebooks on the floor, that had scattered when the stool had fallen into them, was weird. The reason that they'd stood out to me was because the rest of the conservatory was pretty sparse; it didn't have much furniture, or anything else in it. Although now that I knew what I did about Dalton, I understood what was probably in those books. But why would they still be there in the conservatory, so many years after he'd died? Did Penelope and the rest of the family really keep referring to them, when they'd had the chance to move on and be free? And why had there been so many little stools littered all over the floor? Because my memory was now informing me that there had been more than one stool. In fact, there must have been at least six of them, scattered around underneath the lifeless feet of the dead. Did this mean that the Bryants had intentionally killed themselves? That they'd stepped off those stools in order to hang themselves? Although this seemed probable, it just didn't sit right with me. What had happened to them was a mystery, and I had a gut feeling that the Bryant family had met their deaths in a most gruesome and unnatural way. And what that exactly had been, might be too awful to face. I couldn't help thinking that mass suicide hadn't been what had killed them...

CHAPTER SIXTEEN

Jack was still talking, as I was mulling my newly remembered memories around in my mind.

'Of course, Aunt Marjorie knew about Dad channelling God to us, via his notebooks,' Jack was saying. 'Not that she ever properly stepped in and tried to make sure that we were all okay. I can only remember her talking about Dad and his notebooks once, when he had gone away on a business trip, and she'd come to stay the night. That woman likes to pretend she's so perfect, but she's really not. In fact, I'd go as far as to say she's got blood on her hands.'

'Wait,' I said, snapping out of my reverie. 'What? Did you just say that Marjorie actually knew what was going on in your house? That your dad was controlling you all by pretending to get messages from God?'

'Well, I think he was getting some messages from the Lord,' Jack said slowly. 'It's just that he got carried away with it, Ellen. He could see how he could control us effectively by doing this, so it's my belief that he started making up some additional messages of his own, which just isn't right. It's blasphemous, and I'll never forgive him for using us like that.'

'Er, sure,' I said. I knew that there would be no point in entering into a theological debate with my friend right now, about whether or not humans could actually receive messages from God. What was important – as far as I was concerned – was that we both agreed that – at least in part – Dalton's behaviour towards his family had been abusive and controlling. 'I can't believe your aunt actually knew about what he was doing. She was actually enabling his behaviour, Jack, by not doing anything about it. Do you know what I mean?'

'Yep.' Jack's eyebrows lowered, and a scowl spread across his face. I didn't like watching his perfect features scrunch up unpleasantly like that. 'Another weak female; my family is full of them. Granny wasn't any better, she was even more of a doormat than Mum.'

'But,' I said, hoping he wasn't going to go off on a rant against his mother – or grandmother – again, 'what did Marjorie say to you about your dad, and the way he was writing messages in notebooks? Did she have an opinion about it?'

Jack sighed, and shifted position.

'What she said to me went some way to explaining why Dad was doing it,' he said. 'But that still doesn't make his decisions okay. Basically, Aunt Marjorie said that their own father – my grandad – was just as strict as dad, and that he sometimes used to write down instructions for Granny in a notebook, and leave it in the kitchen for her to read. Aunt Marjorie said that Grandad wasn't 'channelling God' with these messages, but just that he was a bad-tempered old git, who wanted things done his way, and that he ruled the house with a rod of iron. He used to tell Granny to serve the meals on time in his notes, and things like that. Granny was from an old established family not far from Buckingham, just up the road in Winslow. She'd been brought up to believe that women were there to serve men, like Mary Magdalene had been to serve Jesus. She believed in this with every fibre of her body, and she brought her children up to believe the same. Aunt Marjorie's way of rebelling was to get on more of an equal footing with Patrick; she's never been subservient to him, as far as I know. Dad must have remembered how his own father treated everyone, and then decided to take it one step further with his own family. Like I said, I really do believe that Dad may have been getting some messages from God; I mean, he was a very devout man, and not all his messages were critical, some were very profound. They made sense. You know? But he took it too far, and started making up messages that he could control us with, and that's where it all went wrong. He should never have done that.'

I nodded, then sat back on the sofa, thinking. This was heavy stuff. And I was becoming more and more aware of a side of Jack that I hadn't seen before this horrible business happened. My best friend really was very religious, that much was clear now. He truly believed in God, and that was strange for me, as I didn't. And I suppose I'd just presumed that most of my friends had the same attitude as me, deep down inside. That religion was a load of mumbo jumbo that didn't actually make sense. That there was so much corruption around that it made it difficult to tell the good religious people from the ones who were in it for the wrong reasons. But clearly, I'd been wrong; the fervour in Jack's eyes when he talked about his Lord told me that much. It didn't put me off him at all, despite the fact that I held differing views to his. In fact, I found his passion attractive, it had such an energy to it. I couldn't help being a bit envious that Jack believed in a higher power to this extent, it must be really comforting for him to have that security, that belief that our existence on earth meant something more than most of us were aware of. I'd tested my own beliefs in God over the years, and to be honest, I always came back with more questions than answers. Like, if there is a loving God, then why do they allow so much suffering in the world? The whole thing seemed a bit fishy to me.

'So Marjorie knew about her brother's way of controlling you all,' I said, crossing my legs. 'It's weird, Jack, that she knew about it yet did nothing to help you. Not really the behaviour of a loving aunt, is it?'

'Yep, I agree,' Jack said, leaning sideways until his head was on my shoulder. 'I just figured it was because their dad – my grandad – had conditioned them to think that that level of control is normal in a family. My dad was just carrying on the tradition in his mind, if you know what I mean. Like I said, I think my aunt has blood on her hands. She could have done something to help us kids, but she chose not to. So in that way she was enabling my father to carry on doing what he was doing. She's really not as perfect as she likes to make out.'

'Hmm,' I said. I wasn't at all convinced by the notion that Jack's dad had simply carried on the notebook thing because he'd seen his own father do it. Dalton had always come across as a very intelligent person, and at some stage he must have wondered if how he was acting was okay. 'But the thing is, you'd have to be really stupid not to realise that controlling your family by writing down negative messages – apparently from God – in order to have power over their thoughts and behaviour, is just plain wrong. And abusive. And your dad was far from stupid, Jack. And Marjorie is an intelligent woman. They must have realised, at some point in time, that Dalton's actions were very wrong and harmful to you all, yet neither of them did anything about it. That's just plain wrong, don't you think?'

'The simple fact is that my family is fucked up, Ellen,' Jack said, his voice coming out low and drawling. 'I've known that for a long time, but I've never properly talked to anyone about it before. I couldn't. But hearing you say these things just makes me realise how bloody wrong everything was.' My heart ached as I watched my friend sit up, lean forwards and then rest his head in his hands. Poor guy, he'd done nothing to deserve the carnage that he'd inherited. I reached out and started rubbing his back, wishing I could take some of his pain away.

'You know, Jack,' I said. 'It's strange. When I first got to know you and Sabrina, I thought you guys were the most perfect examples of the human species that I'd ever met. And then when I met the rest of your family, I was so envious of you all. You all just seemed so beautiful, confident and close knit. I was sure you were all going to be massive successes in life. To be honest, I felt like a dowdy frump next to you all. I had absolutely no clue that your lives were such a nightmare at home, behind closed doors.'

Jack turned his head towards me. I inhaled sharply. He was glaring at me fiercely, his top lip drawn back in a snarl.

'Well it just goes to show, doesn't it Ellen?' he said. I raised my eyebrows, wondering what about my words had caused this change in him. 'That you can't trust the masks that people show to the outside world. The fake niceties. Because people can be master manipulators; they can so easily con you into thinking that everything is hunky-dory and perfect, when it's actually a horrendous fucking shitshow. Be careful of that. Be very wary indeed.'

Jack pushed my tentative hand away, and stood up. My heart sank as I watched him walk off in the direction of his bedroom, coming back a few minutes later, dressed in jeans and a jumper.

'I'm going out,' he said without looking at me. 'I need some fresh air.'

'But it's the middle of the night,' I said, my insides plummeting even further. How on earth had I unwittingly caused such a reaction in my friend? I'd never seen him switch emotions like this. It was like a Jekyll and Hyde thing, the way he'd just switched from being chatty to being hostile. 'It's really dark outside, Jack. We've both had a heavy day. Why don't we both just go back to bed and get some rest?'

But Jack didn't even look at me. I could practically feel the resentment radiating off him. He walked over to the table, grabbed his jacket and phone, then strode over and opened the front door, slamming it loudly behind him. I stared straight ahead, shocked. I felt awful. I couldn't believe that such an innocent thought of mine, spoken aloud, had caused him to react like this. I'd obviously touched a nerve – talking about how his family appeared one way, but was actually another. But why? How? It wasn't like he didn't already know this. He'd never acted like this before. Christ, why was my life suddenly so desperately hard and confusing? Why was Jack treating me like this? I reached over and stroked the cat, finding a bit of comfort from her small, furry body. A wave of sadness rushed through me, and I shut my eyes, wishing that none of this had ever happened. I'd had such a lovely birthday, I'd felt happier than ever on my eighteenth. But now everything was ruined...

CHAPTER SEVENTEEN

M y mind went back to the note that I'd found, the one
Dalton had written that had fallen out of Jack's coat
pocket. There were so many more layers to this family than I'd
ever realised, I thought. It was like peeling back the outer layers
of an onion, to find many more rotten ones hidden beneath the
surface. What the fuck must it have been like, living with
someone who used apparent metaphysical powers to control
you? Jack may believe that God can speak to people, but I was a
hell of a lot more sceptical than him. And I firmly believed that
what Dalton had been doing was child abuse. And that his
family members were brainwashed enough to believe him. Did
that mean that religious fervour was brainwashing? Probably.
But more to the point, the constant criticising from 'God' was a
lot worse.

What had it said on that notepaper? It had talked about the
Lord being unhappy or displeased about Sabrina, and
commanding the rest of the family to make sure she didn't have
access to her phone from the moment she walked through the
door after school. Jesus Christ, the whole family were recruited
to punish each other. It was insane. In the note, Dalton had

gone on to compare his son Jack to the brother that he no longer spoke to, Jacob, which gave me a pretty good idea that he didn't like his son very much. Hadn't he called him insolent? Poor Jack, having a father like that.

Oh God, I thought suddenly. *What if Jack wasn't annoyed with something I'd said, what if he'd stormed off because of something I'd done? Could he somehow know that I'd read the note that had been in his pocket? But how? I'd have to tell him about it, when he came home. I'd always been terrible at keeping secrets...*

CHAPTER EIGHTEEN

I had a dismal couple of hours alone in the flat that night before I went to bed.

At one point my phone pinged, making me jump. Was it Jack, apologising for storming out like that? I leant over and took a look. Christ, it was my brother, Tom. Him texting me was almost unheard of.

Hope you're OK Sis, I read. Mum says you've been through a hard time.

Mum must have told him a bit about what had gone on. I mean, the whole thing was all over the news, too, so Tom would have found out about it sooner or later. He knew Jack, but he'd never liked him. He always said he was a lazy ponce, but then Tom said uncomplimentary things about most people.

Thanks, I texted back. I didn't have the energy to write any more, I was emotionally drained. And I didn't know how much he knew about what had happened. Still, it was nice to know that my angry brother cared enough to send me a message.

My conversation with Jack kept on going round and round in my head. What could I have said that upset him so much? Triggered him to the point where he'd actually stormed out?

The last thing I remembered saying was that I'd been so envious of his family when I was younger. And that I had no idea what they were going through, behind closed doors. *Maybe I touched a nerve with that?* I thought as I washed up our mugs under hot, steamy water. The heat was strangely comforting, as everything else inside me felt icy cold. *Maybe I sounded really insensitive? I mean, Jack would be right in thinking that other people should have noticed something – a sign perhaps – that Dalton was such a tyrant, and done something to help them. Perhaps he's annoyed with me about that, because instead of noticing that he needed help, I just envied him in a really ignorant way? Yes,* I decided, *that must be it. And who could blame him? I would probably feel the same way if I'd been in his shoes. Desperately wanting help, but unable to ask for it, and no one around me doing anything productive. He must have felt so let down and abandoned by everyone. Including me.*

As I picked up a tea towel, a memory of Sabrina popped into my mind. We'd just done our GCSEs at school, and the rest of the year – including me – were beyond joyful, because it meant that we would have a longer summer holiday than everyone else in the school, because once you'd done your last exam, you were allowed to stay at home on 'study leave' for the rest of the summer term. Year 11 had been having an unofficial party that day in a corner of the school grounds. People had brought in sweets, chocolates and drinks to share, and Adam had even sneaked in a bottle of vodka, which everyone was taking sips out of. Several people were smoking, but I wasn't, it's never been my thing. I tried it once, and it made me choke. Maybe I was just born a bit square. At one point during the party, needing the loo, I'd slipped away – and no one noticed, because as usual I was on the edge of the fun, sitting on the outskirts of the throng – and made my way up to the main building. On my way to the toilets, I heard crying coming from one of the classrooms. I popped my head round the door, and found Sabrina in there, all alone, sobbing as though her heart was going to break. She'd obviously been there a while, as her face already had that red, blotchy look.

'Oh Sabrina,' I said, going up to her and hugging her tightly. 'What on earth is wrong?' I felt a bit bad at that point, as I hadn't even noticed that she hadn't been with all of us at the bottom of the sports field. But I was already obsessed with her brother by that point, and didn't have room in my head to think of much else. Although we weren't so close anymore, it still disturbed me to see her so upset, and my natural inclination was to try to find out what was wrong.

Sabrina couldn't answer me for a while, she was too consumed by whatever grief she was suffering. I remember watching as she sobbed, then nearly stopped, and then was overtaken by a fresh wave of emotion. Eventually she drew away from me and I stared with sadness at her distraught, swollen face.

'This means I'm going to have to be at home full time for ages.' She sniffed. 'Now that the exams are over.'

'Yeah, but isn't that a good thing?' I said – stupid, ignorant young girl that I was. Personally, I'd been looking forward to lazing around for a long time. Tom was still at home then, and I knew that he would be a pain in my arse, with all his arguing and shouting, but I was used to him. I couldn't wait to lie around in bed all day, or watch rubbish on TV. 'You can have loads of lie-ins, and not worry about homework for months.'

But Sabrina just shook her head furiously and stepped away from me.

'You don't understand,' she said fiercely, sobs taking her over again. 'You just don't understand. No one understands.'

Now, at the time, I was a bit offended by the way she acted that day. Myabe offended is the wrong word. I was a bit upset that she'd been so hostile in her reaction to my words. Because I had no idea what she was referring to, and I'd tried to be kind to her, but felt rejected by her. But I never forgot that conversation, every now and again I would mull it over in my mind, trying to make sense of it. I already knew that her father was strict, but I had no idea of the living hell he no doubt made her life in the summer after her GCSEs. I now doubt very much whether she was able to have any lie-ins at all. God only knows what messages were being written about her in those damned notebooks. I still couldn't wrap my head around how Dalton could have done that to her and the rest of them. Even a man with a need to control everyone must have some sort of inner moral compass? And now the poor girl was dead. I couldn't even ask her. Her life was gone and nothing could bring it back. And if I'd clicked that day, if I'd just looked into what she meant more, maybe I could have done something to help her. Or I could have told a teacher, who would no doubt have connected Sabrina with the right people who could help her. Why oh why did she never tell a teacher herself? I already knew the answer to that; she would have been too scared that nothing much would be done, and that she would have to continue living with her father, and that his punishments towards her would go off the scale after he found out that she'd told on him. God, if only I could turn back time...

CHAPTER NINETEEN

I woke up early on Monday morning, another nightmare about being hung from the ceiling jolting me into consciousness. I reached up and felt my neck, and then wiped a thin layer of sweat from my forehead. Would I ever be able to get past the horror of everything that had happened? Be able to somehow put all of this in the past and move on? Shit, I really didn't want to crack up. I couldn't afford to, then I would be no help to Jack at all. I had to somehow keep a certain calmness in my head. I leaned over and checked my alarm clock; it was 5.47am.

I needed to go and check on my friend, I decided. I was sure that Jack would have come back from his late-night walk; I'd had to go back to bed after he'd left as I was so tired. But I fell asleep pretty sure that he would let himself back into the flat at some point, and that I'd hear him snoring in his room when I woke up. I stayed still for a second, listening for the usual grunts and snores. Everything in the flat was silent. The only sounds coming to my ears were the dulled traffic noises from outside, and the muffled sounds of people chatting in the street.

Chandos Road, where I lived, was always full of human traffic, as it connected the locals with many places where they'd need to be; two schools, the university, a pub and a park. Hmm, that was strange. Jack was never a morning person, and with the amount he'd drunk the day before, I was expecting him to snooze right through to the afternoon.

It was late October – nearly Halloween – and so far I'd got away with not putting the heating on. Trying to save money, and all that – I was a student after all. Having low bills would certainly help me out, as my student loan would only stretch so far. But, I reflected, as I stood up and dragged a thick hoodie out of a drawer, before pulling it over my head – my dressing gown still presumably being in Jack's bedroom – I might have to turn it on soon. The air felt icy that morning, and I was shivering as I slipped my feet into my slippers, then made my way out of my bedroom and across the narrow hallway to Jack's room. His door was ajar. I pushed it open, looked inside, and stopped. The room was empty. Jack's bed was in the exact state as it had been yesterday and my dressing gown was in a heap on the floor. His desk was the usual mess that it always was, his laptop – closed – surrounded by scribbled-on sheets of paper. Okay, strange. Was he somewhere else in the flat, perhaps?

A thorough search of the small space revealed the fact that – apart from Nala, who was now also up and ready for the day – I was on my own in there. Jack must have never come home last night. A pang of fear ricocheted through me. Where would he have gone? To his aunt and uncle's house, maybe? That seemed an unlikely outcome, considering how drunk/hungover he'd been when he'd left, and how conservative those two were, how intolerant of any vices. He was so vulnerable at the moment, and after last night's outburst – so sensitive and volatile. Which was completely understandable given what he was going through. *Oh shit*, I thought. *Has he gone and done something stupid? Harmed himself? Or worse...* After all, hadn't he been saying that he didn't know how he was going to get through this nightmare yesterday, before we'd gone to the pub? If he had, it would be my fault, for inadvertently saying something that had upset him. Christ, if I could just learn to be a bit more tactful...

Going back into my room and dressing myself hastily, I knew I had to find my friend and check that he was okay. I quickly fed the cat, changed her litter tray and topped up her water. My heart beating fast, I grabbed a bottle of juice, my handbag and keys, and stepped out of my flat into the communal hall, and then out on to the street. It was still dark. Monday mornings were always busy and bustling in Buckingham, and even at this early hour the binmen were out and about, and several cars were flowing up and down my road. *Where should I look first?* I wondered. *If I were Jack, where would I have gone last night?*

I set off in the direction of the high street, checking each and every doorway that I saw; my thinking with that being that he might have gone and found more alcohol, and then passed out somewhere while he was trying to find his way home. That he might have done something terrible to himself, and need urgent medical help. Nothing. I made my way round the corner of the Hat and Hare pub, past the town hall, and down into the main shop-lined road that was the hub of Buckingham. The first glimmers of daylight were shimmering through the clouds behind the buildings now, but it was bloody cold, and I pulled my coat tighter round me, wishing I'd been clever enough to bring a scarf and hat.

As I passed the newsagent, I saw piles of bound newspapers. I stopped and took a quick look at the one on the top. *Murder or Suicide?* I read.

The Echo has learned that police are still unsure whether the six people found hanging met their untimely demise through a tragic group suicide, or whether a crime took place in their house...

I stopped reading and walked on. I couldn't focus on any more details about the case right now, I needed to find Jack. He was alive, hopefully, and he was my priority. And seeing the Bryants' heart-breaking deaths made into sensational fodder for the masses made me feel rather sick.

When I'd finished my trawl past the coffee shops, charity shops, restaurants, banks, and various other assorted businesses that filled this area, a thought suddenly came to me. The graveyard. Jack often took me there when we'd had a beer, it was one of his favourite places in the area. It was just behind the tall church of St Peter and St Paul on the hill that dominated Buckingham town, a beautiful, tree-filled spot that had been there for hundreds of years. No fresh graves had been put there for ages, as the space had all been filled up a long time ago. Which meant the resulting area had a peaceful air about it of times gone by. Wild flowers lined the sides, the branches of old trees brushed the grass, and it was a popular spot with dog walkers in the daytime and teenagers at night. As I turned and walked up Castle Street towards the spire, with more people coming out of their houses and getting into their cars, I hoped fervently that I would find him there.

As I rounded the church and walked down the narrow path towards the graveyard – which had the privilege of being a hedged-in space with a gate for access – I wished the sun's rays would hurry up and illuminate the area a bit more. While the high street had had a fair amount of traffic and people about, the area around the church was a different story. It was completely deserted. And although I usually found it beautiful during daylight hours, now I was finding it eerie, a spooky grey area that reminded me of the horror films my brother Tom had forced me to watch with him. The potential for danger here suddenly felt very real, I was an eighteen-year-old girl on my own, no one in the whole world knew that I'd come here. What if there was a person about here who wanted to harm someone? Harm me? My footsteps quickened, and I resolved to do the quickest search of the graveyard that I possibly could, before returning to the safety of the busier streets. Luckily there was the soft glow of the odd street lamp illuminating the area, which made things a bit better, although it also made the shadows appear even darker...

As I pushed the gate to the graveyard open, I saw them there, illuminated by the orange light of a lamp post. Jack and that bitch Layla, slumped on top of each other on a bench, their arms and legs entangled. Beer cans and an empty bottle of gin lay at their feet. I was so stunned that I couldn't move. My instinct was to get out of there before they saw me, but I was rooted to the spot. I was standing less than ten metres away from the two of them; after all, it wasn't a big graveyard.

It was Layla who turned her head and saw me first.

'Oh look who it is,' she said, her speech slurred. 'Boring Ellen. Come to spy on Jack, have you? You don't like letting him out of your sight for a second, do you?'

'I–' was all I could manage. For the most part, I wanted the grass beneath my feet to open up and swallow me. But an anger had sparked in my heart too, caused by the sight of them so lazily collapsed on top of each other. So Jack had slept with me yesterday – whether I could remember it or not wasn't the point – and now he was entangled in a lustful heap with Layla? I mean, for God's sake, his family had just died. Was this really how people behaved when they were grieving? And Layla, of all people to see him with. It was too much to bear.

Jack turned, shifting position until he was staring right at me. He was almost unrecognisable, a wreck of his usual self. But he was grinning in a way that made me want to cry.

'Morning, Ellen,' he said. 'Layla and I were feeling a bit cold, so we decided to cosy up. You know how it is.'

Layla laughed when he said this, then bent her head down and kissed the tip of his nose.

'We've done a bit more than that,' she said with a giggle. 'Eh, Jack?'

I couldn't watch or listen anymore.

'I just wanted to check that you were all right, Jack,' I said. Just getting those words out made my throat hurt. 'I can see that you are.'

I turned and walked back out of the graveyard, desperately trying to ignore the sniggering that was coming from the bench.

My head was reeling as I headed back towards my flat. My cheeks were burning with what – shame? But why should I have to feel ashamed, I wondered, blinking away hot tears. What had I done wrong, other than try to make sure that my best friend was safe?

Best friend. That was an interesting phrase, I thought, making my way to Chandos Road. Was Jack actually my friend? Did friends treat each other like this? So carelessly? I mean, I'd come to terms with the fact that he didn't have the same feelings for me as I did for him. But we shared a flat, we were close, and he was always saying what a good friend I was to him. And we'd slept together. I was hoping that would change things, make us closer, but I'd been aware that it might not, that it might have been a one-time deal. We'd both been so drunk. But to then storm out of the flat and end up with that bitch Layla on a park bench? It just seemed so callous. Did he actually care that his family was dead? Finished off in such a brutally awful way, whether it be from suicide or murder? At this moment in time, I felt like I was grieving their loss more than him. I felt cut up inside, desperate, filled with a horror that I never knew could exist. But Jack? He was laughing, drinking, and cuddling Layla on a park bench. What the actual fuck?

CHAPTER TWENTY

I stomped back through Buckingham towards my flat, glaring at anyone who dared to make eye contact with me. *I'm sorry,* I thought, *but Jack has a very strange way of grieving.* Apart from anything else and excluding the fact that I'd just seen the man I loved being given a kiss by an arch bitch, who the hell acts like he has been when their whole family has just died? I mean, I get that people react differently to grief, but half the time Jack just didn't seem to care that his mum, granny, brother and sisters had been found dead. That he'd seen them hanging there with his own eyes. I mean, at the time, he'd collapsed on the floor of the Bryants' house, and had been a catatonic mess for the rest of the day. But all he'd wanted to do after that was get drunk and sleep with me, and probably Layla. It was too much for me to process. I knew how differently I would have reacted if it had been my own family that we'd found that day. I just couldn't relate to Jack's behaviour. It was beyond odd.

I rounded the corner of the town hall. More and more people were out and about, and it was quite light now. The traffic was getting heavier, and lots of vans were stopping by shops to unload their wares. I didn't know what to do with myself now. It had been such a surprise to find Layla and Jack there like that. And to think, I'd actually been worried about him. What a fucking joke.

Shouldn't we be worrying about more important things right now? Like who killed the whole of his family, rather than which girl he wants to mess around with? For God's sake, the whole situation was becoming ludicrous now. If this was Jack's way of dealing with unbearable grief, then there wasn't much I was going to be able to do about his behaviour. But what I wanted to know was what actually happened to the Bryants. More specifically, who was responsible for their deaths...

CHAPTER TWENTY-ONE

Then an unpleasant memory popped into my mind. *Shit*, I thought. *That's weird, I haven't thought about this for years. Blocked it out more like...*

Although I'd spent the last several years idolising Jack, and thinking that he was literally the most perfect human specimen that I'd ever come across, there had been an occasion when he'd really hurt my feelings. Sabrina and I were fourteen, and were both in the school play. I was in the chorus, and had to dress up in an old-fashioned dress. My mum had spent ages doing my hair – curling it into ringlets, and although I usually didn't have much confidence in my looks, that evening – as I gazed at my reflection in my mum's wardrobe mirror – I thought I was looking pretty snappy. More attractive than usual. I was wearing a long fitted dress made from indigo-coloured silk that we'd found in a charity shop, and it seemed to bring out the colour of my eyes, and complement my hair. At least, that's what I'd initially thought.

But when we'd got to school, and met Jack and Sabrina in the corridor outside the hall, my newly found self-esteem soon drained away. Jack took one look at me and then his nose screwed up and he let out a loud snigger, before turning and marching back into the hall.

'Oh, just ignore him,' Sabrina said. She was looking like a perfect princess of course, dressed in a pale-turquoise gown that made her hair look even blonder. 'I don't know what's got into him this evening.'

But the damage had been done. Jack had mocked my outfit, he'd clearly thought I looked ridiculous; terrible. As the teacher called us both to come backstage, a burning wave of shame swept through me, and I wanted to tear my stupid dress off and wash the bloody ringlets out of my hair. I'd always felt so body conscious, but that day I'd actually felt attractive – up until Jack had seen me, anyway. And in my heart of hearts, maybe I'd wanted him to think so, too. But he'd clearly felt the opposite, that I looked ridiculous. It took me weeks to shake off that feeling of shame, but everything had miraculously fixed itself the next time I'd seen Jack and he'd been back to his normal, charming self again, making me feel so important when I was talking to him. It was as though he'd never sniggered at my dress, and made me feel like such a frumpy, unattractive mess. So eventually I blocked the incident out, and never thought of it again. Until now. And now that I remembered this horrible incident, another one was at the back of my mind... Jack had done something a lot worse once, I could feel it. This was a disturbing notion, as though some ominous memory was trying to make itself known. But for now, whatever it was wouldn't come completely forward.

CHAPTER TWENTY-TWO

S od *this,* I thought, walking up the path to the communal door of the flats. I needed some space, someplace where I knew Jack wouldn't be. When I'd seen him there on the bench with Layla, a thought had come to me. *Do you really know this man at all? Did you ever expect him to do something like this to you?* I needed some time to think. I was going to go to my mum's. It's where I always went when I was feeling low or in pain.

Half an hour later I was outside my mum's small semi, ringing the bell. As she opened the front door, she was rubbing her eyes.

'Oh hello love,' she said. 'It's very early.' She looked at me, taking my terrible state in. Her expression quickly changed. 'Ellen, are you all right? You look awful. Come in.'

Soon we were sitting on the sofa, cups of tea in our hands, with me pouring everything out about Jack; how he was behaving, the fact that I'd thought we were getting closer – I didn't tell her we'd had sex, Christ I don't want to talk to my mum about that sort of thing – but that he'd stormed off and not come home last night. That I'd found him drunk in

Buckingham's graveyard with that hussy Layla not more than half an hour ago. That it hadn't been a very pleasant experience, and that I'd felt like they were laughing at me. That I was now questioning how well I knew Jack at all. That it was making me feel even worse than I already had been, after everything that had happened, after what we'd seen on Saturday morning... I didn't tell her that a nasty memory at the back of my mind was trying to come forward, and that I had a feeling that it involved Jack. Until I remembered exactly what it was, I wasn't planning on saying anything to anyone about it.

'Mum,' I said, turning to her. My head was feeling very heavy – partly grief and sadness, and partly hangover. 'If I ask you something please will you give me a truthful answer?'

'Yes, love.' My mum nodded her head. 'Of course.'

Good, I knew I could trust her. I paused, thinking about the right way to phrase it.

'The other day, you were talking about Jack's family being complicated,' I said. 'You were saying something about things not always being as perfect on the inside as they look on the outside. Afterwards, when I thought about what you were saying, it seemed like you might know more about the Bryants than you're telling me? I could really do with a heads-up now, Mum. Do you know some things about them that you haven't told me yet?'

My mum looked at me, then sighed.

'Okay, love,' she said. 'There is a little bit more that I've heard about them, but I didn't tell you because you usually get so annoyed when I say anything about that family.'

I didn't say anything because what she said was true. I nodded instead.

'And also all I know is hearsay, from the locals, you know?' she went on. 'I don't know how much of this is true, and how much is gossip. But you know what they say, there's usually no smoke without fire.'

I fought back the urge to roll my eyes at this proverb. It was so typical of Mum to back up her beliefs with some popular saying or other.

'Go on,' I said.

'Well.' Mum was sounding more confident now, probably because I hadn't reacted as I usually did when she insinuated that all might not be perfect with the Bryants. But then, after everything Jack had recently told me, I now knew she was right about this. Maybe I should have listened to her warnings before...

'Mrs Parker – you know, the older lady who wears the red beret – and I often have a chat when we bump into each other in town,' Mum went on. 'I know her from when we used to go to church, she's a nice lady. Anyway, she's told me a few things over the years about that family. I never told you what she was saying, because like I said, I didn't want you to kick off, and I wasn't sure how much truth there was in her tales. But certain things she's told me do give me pause for thought.'

'Like what?' I said.

'Well,' Mum said, sitting back and getting more comfortable. 'After Dalton passed away, Mrs Parker told me that once she'd heard crying coming from the Bryants' garden – a few months previously. She said that the sound had seemed so anguished, that she felt compelled to investigate in case someone was in trouble. So she knocked on the front door and rang the bell, but no one answered. So she went back to the fence, and found a gap between two of the panels, and peered through, hoping to see who it was that was upset. That's when she spotted Penelope, curled up into a little ball at the side of the patio, sobbing her heart out, and rocking herself backwards and forwards.'

I shook my head, feeling sad.

'Poor Penelope,' I said. 'She was going through so much, and none of us realised.'

Mum nodded.

'But that's not the strangest part,' she said. 'Mrs Parker said that the oddest bit was that Dalton was there too, and was calmly doing some gardening, not far away from his wife. He knew perfectly well that she was in bits, but was completely ignoring her. So cold and callous of him.'

I thought back to what Jack said about his Mum being a doormat. It seemed a harsh conclusion to come to, given how his dad treated her. I mean, I wasn't exactly a psychologist or anything, but even I knew that an abusive person could wear away another person's sense of self, if they tried hard enough. And surely that's what had happened with Penelope?

'I know, it's really sad,' I said with a sigh. 'Jack's told me a bit about how his dad treated his mum. But that's common knowledge, Mum. Mrs Parker spread the word around about Dalton's behaviour after he died, didn't she? Most people in Buckingham have second- or third-hand knowledge about it by now.'

'Yes.' My mother eyed me beadily. 'But what she hasn't told many people, is that she continued to see Penelope being distraught long after Dalton had died.'

I blinked.

'Mrs Parker told me that there was a brief time when Penelope seemed happier, after her husband had passed away,' Mum said. 'That for a couple of months or so, the lines on her forehead relaxed a bit, and she didn't seem so worn out. She even smiled a couple of times. But then one day, all that changed. And eventually Penelope stopped making contact with Mrs Parker altogether, if they saw each other on the street. In fact, apparently she rarely went anywhere in the end; she

SARAH SHERIDAN

mostly just stayed in her house for some reason. And although the younger kids went off to school, they always came home straight away, and never seemed to have any friends over or anything. Not like when Sabrina was younger, and you were there all the time. Mrs Parker is lovely, but she is a bit nosy, and she was keeping an eye on the house from her living-room window. In her eyes, she was doing her bit for neighbourhood watch.'

I sat, thinking for a minute. Now this was strange news. I mean, I could totally understand why poor Penelope would be upset when Dalton was around, because he'd apparently been so cruel to her. But after he'd gone, why on earth would she go from recovering and seeming happier, to suddenly upset and hermit-like again? It didn't make sense. Although, maybe Jack was right. Perhaps his mum had been psychologically weak in some way, and just didn't have the resilience to cope with life, even when no one around her was hurting her? It was something we'd probably never know now. The image of Penelope's body hanging from the conservatory flashed through my mind, and I shivered. Would I ever get over what I'd seen that morning? Probably not, I reflected. How the fuck did you get over something so awful and sad, so horrific and grotesque?

'Are you okay, love?' Mum was peering at me, a worried expression on her face. 'You've gone as white as a sheet.'

'Yeah,' I said. 'I'm fine, just feeling a bit run-down at the moment. And sad about the Bryants.'

Mum nodded, reaching out to give my hands a squeeze.

My mobile phone, which was lying on the coffee table in front of us, jumped into life. I looked at it and saw Jack's name flashing up.

'Er,' I said, suddenly feeling a wave of guilt about talking about him to my mum. Had I gone a bit overboard? I wondered.

Was I making something out of nothing here? 'I might just go upstairs to answer this.'

My mum had seen his name too. She didn't look all that happy, but she just nodded her head and took a sip of her tea.

I grabbed my phone and legged it upstairs into my old room, which was next to Tom's. This man had some sort of magnetic hold over me, I was thinking as I closed the door. Even when I was annoyed with him, I couldn't help answering his calls. Can people exude a kind of power over others? Because if they could, then Jack definitely had that skill.

'Jack?' I said, pressing the green button.

'Ellen,' Jack said. As soon as I heard his husky voice, my heart melted, despite my better judgement. 'Why did you leave so quickly when you found me and Layla in the graveyard?' He sounded quite hurt. I found myself immediately questioning my reaction that morning. Had I overreacted? Been a bit silly? Read too much into the situation? I was probably overtired, I thought. I mean, I'd been through a lot too, and we'd got horrendously drunk yesterday.

'Sorry,' I found myself saying. 'I-I just thought you two might want to be alone.' I remembered how heartbroken and betrayed I'd felt seeing the two of them in a heap on the bench. Could I have got it all wrong?

Jack laughed.

'We were just messing around,' he said, as though spending the night with Layla had meant absolutely nothing to him at all. 'When I left the flat, I was feeling upset about my family and didn't feel ready to sleep. So I kept walking, and bumped into Layla outside The Crown. We just hung out and talked for a while, and yes, had a few beers, so we had a kiss and a cuddle. That was all, Ellen.'

He chuckled again, and suddenly I felt really embarrassed.

'Oh,' I said. 'Cool. I'm glad you found someone to talk to last night. Of course you must be feeling upset; your whole family has just died. You must be in unimaginable pain. Sorry for just walking off, Jack. I'm a bit tired today, maybe that's affecting my judgement.'

'No worries at all, old bean,' my friend said. 'Listen, are you coming back to the flat soon? The police have just phoned with the autopsy results, and listening to all the details has fucked my head up a bit. I'd really like to talk it over with you, but not on the phone. Do you have university or can you come back here for a while?'

I looked at the time in the top corner of my phone. I should really be going to a lecture, but Jack had just received the autopsy results for his family, so there was no way I could let him down right now.

'It's fine,' I said, a relief washing through me that our friendship was back on track. He did like and value me after all, otherwise why would he choose me to talk to about the results? 'I'm just at my mum's. I'll leave now, Jack. I won't be long.'

I jogged back down the stairs, catching sight of myself in the mirror on the way. Jesus, I looked awful. Blotchy face, no make-up, hair a mess. Oh well, I couldn't do much about that now, could I? Jack would have to take me as I was.

'Mum,' I said. 'I've got to go.'

'Has Jack summoned you then, Ellen? He just has to click his fingers and you come running, don't you?' she said – a definite scathing edge to her voice.

'He's just had the autopsy results back for his family,' I said, a sharpness entering my tone. Part of me knew that I was reacting in an unfair way, given everything I'd said to her about Jack when I'd first arrived. But I didn't want to be reminded of my fickleness, of the magnetic force I felt pulling me to him. 'So I said I'd go and talk them through with him.'

My mum exhaled. She suddenly looked very weary.

'Okay, love,' she said. 'But I hadn't finished telling you everything that Mrs Parker told me about the Bryants. There was one more thing, which might be important...'

'I'll phone you later, Mum,' I said, turning and heading for the front door. 'I promise. Thanks for the tea.'

Minutes later, I was walking back into town, heading for my little flat in Chandos Road. While I walked I was trying to shake away the image of my mum's face as I'd said goodbye to her. She'd looked so down. I wasn't exactly sure why. I mean, I got that she'd wanted to say more to me, and that I'd just been complaining about Jack to her, so she might think it was strange that I was off to see him so quickly. But surely she'd understand how volatile people could be when they were grieving? I'd overreacted after seeing him with Layla this morning, I knew that now. Just a bit of old-fashioned jealousy. But why had Mum looked so worried when I'd turned to wave at her? Maybe her depression was getting worse. Perhaps I should suggest that she go and speak to the doctor about it?

CHAPTER TWENTY-THREE

A memory of Mum – about two weeks after Dad had left, when I was twelve – flooded my mind. I'd come in one day from school, and found her just sobbing and sobbing, sitting at the kitchen table. I don't know why, but it had really irritated me – seeing her like this. I'd been in pain at the time too, but I'd just got on with life, forced myself to keep smiling, going off to school every day. But Mum just seemed to be falling apart. I'd caught her with a tear-stained face a few times, but this was the first time I'd actually seen her in hysterics. And it scared me. Because now that Dad had moved out and I hardly ever saw him, I knew that she was my primary caregiver. And if she fell apart, then so would I...

'What's wrong, Mum?' I'd said, putting my bag on a chair. I just wanted her to shut up and go back to normal, and make the dinner or something. Do anything, rather than sob.

'Oh hello, love,' Mum had said through her sobs. 'I'm so sorry, Ellen, but I can't stop crying.'

I'd stood there next to her, feeling beyond awkward. *I'm not a good daughter,* I remember thinking at the time. *Because if I was, I'd put my arms around her and console her.* But I couldn't do that. I just wanted her to pull herself together again and be strong. I felt afraid and repelled by her behaviour.

I'd stayed there for ages, watching Mum's shoulders shake, listening to her snort and cry. The irritation of the whole thing had grown in me, bit by bit, because she just wouldn't stop. In the end, I'd grabbed my bag and stormed off to my room, slamming the door behind me. *Penelope would never act like that*, I remember thinking. *She'd never make such a spectacle of herself.*

But now I knew different, didn't I? Penelope had been going through a bad time – a horrific time – at home, but she'd never told anyone about it.

At least my mum was honest with her emotions. And now, with everything that had happened, and especially after seeing how much Penelope's inability to share what was going on with her had stopped people being able to perhaps intervene and halt the impending tragedy that killed the Bryants, I felt guilty about leaving my mum that day. Felt awful about being irritated with her and walking off like that. If I could redo it, and go back in time, I knew that I would now put my arms around her and give her the biggest hug. But the problem was that none of us could go back in time and fix things. However badly we might want to...

CHAPTER TWENTY-FOUR

As I walked back to my little flat in Chandos Road – one of the oldest roads in Buckingham, apparently it had been around for over a hundred years – I mulled over my one-sided relationship with Jack. Because it did feel like a relationship – at least to me – because my feelings for him had evolved to the point of being overwhelmingly strong, and I went through the ups and downs that people in actual relationships did, depending on how well we were getting on. When he was pleased with me, or said something kind, my heart soared, and I loved being with him. I would walk around feeling elated all day. When he was annoyed with me, or distant, I became an emotional wreck, constantly ruminating on what I'd said or done wrong, and hoping against hope that we would soon be back in a good place. Part of me knew that it wasn't entirely healthy to have my emotions dependent on someone else's reactions like this, but I couldn't help it. If I'm honest, I think Jack was totally oblivious to all this. From his perspective, we were friends and he lived in my spare room. Albeit rent free, but that didn't bother me.

I remember how I'd been so taken with him, the first time I'd ever seen him, while he'd been up that tree in the Bryants' garden. He'd seemed to glow with some sort of effervescent energy, which blew me away, as I'd never felt like I ever exuded that sort of magnetic force. I'd been addicted from the start. As we'd got older, I found myself seeking out his company – overhearing where he was likely to be, then accidentally on purpose turning up at that place myself. I tried to make myself more and more attractive as we grew up, hoping that maybe one day he would see me as more than just a friend. I lost a bit of weight, bought myself some new clothes with my savings, and learned how to apply make-up in a way that didn't make me look too horrific.

'Blimey Ellen,' my mum said one day, as I was on my way to university. 'You're turning into a bit of a stunner. Watch out boys, here she comes…'

But I'd never felt like a beautiful person or anything, not next to Sabrina and all the other pretty girls in the class. I thought Mum was duty bound to say that kind of thing as she loved me and was my parent, so I never took her words very seriously. Although I did notice that the boys gradually started paying me more attention at school.

Hopefully, I thought, as I walked along, this was just another little blip – me finding Jack and Layla lying together – and everything would all sort itself out again. Hopefully the feeling of crippling insecurity that had pumped through me as soon as I'd seen them lying together on that park bench would soon go. And I would be back to being Jack's closest, trusted ally. I did hope he would be in a good mood when I got home…

CHAPTER TWENTY-FIVE

'Hello?' I called, closing my front door behind me. 'Jack?'

I walked into the living room. There he was, curled up on the sofa with a mug of steaming coffee in his hands, Nala the cat snuggled up next to him, snoozing happily. He'd had a shower, I could tell that from the scent of soap that pervaded the room, and the fact that his hair was still wet. He looked so calm, almost serene, sitting there. As though the previous twenty-four hours just hadn't happened. Which struck me as kind of odd.

'There you are,' he said, as though it had been me who'd been missing all night. As I looked at him, a whole melting pot of emotions rushed through me. Relief, at seeing that he was okay. The usual overpowering love that I had for him, which literally made my knees go weak. Anger and hurt, because – whatever he said about Layla, what I'd seen in the graveyard had really affected me. Embarrassment, in case he was right about me overreacting. I decided that the best thing to do, to distract myself from this tumult of emotion, was to go over to the kitchenette and make myself a strong cup of tea.

'Come and sit with me when you've done that, Ellen,' Jack called. 'There's something that I think we need to discuss.'

Oh God, I thought. *He's going to tell me about the autopsies. I'm not sure I can handle hearing about the gory details, but I suppose I'm going to have to...*

I took the tea bag out, slung it in the food recycling bin, chucked some milk into my mug, picked it up and then slowly walked over and positioned myself on the armchair.

'What do you want to talk about?' I said, after taking a sip of tea.

Jack smiled, then brushed his forehead with his hand.

'Er, this is rather awkward, old bean,' he said, looking rueful. 'I don't really know how to bring it up, so I'll just come out and say it. Yesterday, when we were both drunk, you told me – in quite a lot of detail – about the feelings you have for me.'

An electric feeling of what? – shock? shame? hideous embarrassment? – rocketed through me. Had I? I racked my brains, but so much of the day before was a blank. I wasn't used to drinking that much alcohol – whereas Jack was – so no wonder he could remember stuff that I couldn't. Oh God, how cringey. I'd promised myself that I'd never tell him how I felt. And here he was in front of me, telling me that I'd gone and blurted it all out. And I'd thought he was going to discuss his family's autopsies...

'Oh,' I managed, feeling a hot blush spread over my face. 'What, er, did I say, exactly?'

Jack flashed his perfect teeth at me again.

'No need to feel embarrassed, Ellen,' he said, staring at my burning cheeks. 'I took it all as a compliment. It was really sweet of you. Basically, you told me that you'd been in love with me for several years now, and that you knew I probably didn't like you in the same way, but that you just liked living with me and being near me, as it was better than not seeing me at all.'

The red-hot shame doubled in its intensity. I just wanted the armchair to open up and swallow me whole. What a dickhead I was, to admit this to Jack the minute I had some drink in me. How awful and mortifying. Him knowing how I felt would no doubt change everything between us. We could no longer carry on as 'best friends', because he would know that the relationship was unequal, and that I wanted our friendship to be more than that. Oh God, why oh why had I opened my stupid pissed mouth and told him? And what made it worse, was that I couldn't bloody remember even having that conversation with him. That period of time was a complete blank to me.

'Oh well,' I said with a huge sigh. 'Might as well ask you outright then, Jack, as I don't have anything to lose at this point. Do you have any stronger feelings for me than just friendship? It's something I've been wondering for a while. I won't mind if you say no,' I added quickly. 'It's just that I'd rather know for certain, one way or another.'

Jack gazed at me for a second or two, then waggled his eyebrows up and down.

'I do really like you, Ellen,' he said. 'You must know that. I mean, the thing is, that I'm going through a lot right now, with everyone in my family dying. My head's all over the place. To be honest, it's something we should probably discuss a bit further down the line, if that's all right with you? I know we shagged yesterday, and that was great. But at the moment I'm just not in the right headspace to talk about relationships. Do you understand what I mean?'

'Oh God, of course,' I blurted out, immediately telling myself off for being so insensitive. 'I totally understand, Jack. I'm sorry, I shouldn't have asked, it was the wrong time.'

'That's okay,' he said, shifting position. 'I just wanted to let you know what you'd said when we were pissed, as best friends don't have any secrets from each other, do they?'

'No.' I gave a little grin. I was suddenly feeling very small inside, like I'd unwittingly been making his life a lot harder, without realising it. And hadn't he just said that he really liked me? What did that actually mean? Obviously, I couldn't ask him to explain what he meant, as now clearly wasn't the right time. But had he meant in a romantic way or a friendship way? I found it so hard to read him.

'So, the autopsy results.' Jack leant forwards and placed his mug on the coffee table. His face, I noticed, had suddenly become very serious.

'Yes?' I said. 'What were they?' I braced myself for whatever it was that I was about to hear.

Jack exhaled.

'This is so hard to talk about,' he said. 'But I need to tell someone. Basically, the coroner has ruled the deaths of my family to be a mass suicide.'

'Really?' I said. I was genuinely surprised at this. The sight of them had been so horrific and unexpected, that it just didn't seem feasible that the Bryants had decided to take their lives together. I mean, the act of a group suicide seemed just totally unfathomable. And I'd had such a horrifically eerie feeling when I'd seen them altogether. Sabrina had been my friend, well, I hadn't been such a good friend to her recently, but I still cared about her a lot. And the Sabrina that I knew would never have just decided to end her life like that. I'd honestly thought that foul play was involved, that some sort of crime had taken place.

'Yeah,' Jack breathed, looking down. 'It's as I suspected, Ellen. Do you remember I told you I thought it was suicide?'

I nodded. Jack obviously knew his family better than anyone. It made sense that he would have guessed the cause of their deaths. But still, something about that verdict didn't sit right with me, and I couldn't put my finger exactly on why that was...

CHAPTER TWENTY-SIX

We spent a good few hours mulling over the coroner's conclusion, with Nala sleeping soundly throughout our discussion. Me questioning it, wondering how they could have just ignored the fact that it was such a strange thing to happen – six members of a family found hanging all at once. Jack standing by the ruling, saying that he'd known that's what had happened all along.

I kept asking Jack if he was okay. I couldn't help putting myself in his shoes, and I knew that if the same thing had happened to my family, I would feel absolutely destroyed, like I couldn't carry on. It would annihilate me. But the thing that was confusing me about my friend was that his emotional state seemed to jump all over the place. One minute he was sad and serious, the next minute he was laughing and joking. But I'd heard somewhere that people all grieve differently, so I just figured that this was Jack's way of dealing with his loss. There was no handbook that came with this type of trauma after all. If there was, I would have gone out and bought a copy by now...

'Jack,' I said, as I placed our fifth cups of tea on the coffee table. 'There's something I have to tell you. When I was clearing up the room a couple of days ago, a piece of paper fell out of your jacket pocket. I didn't want to read it or anything,' I said hurriedly. 'But it fell open, and as I picked it up I saw that it was a page out of a notebook. I think it was one that your dad had written. I just wanted to tell you that I'd seen it, because like you said before, best friends don't keep secrets from one another.' Okay, so I hadn't told the complete truth, and I hoped my cheeks weren't going red again because of this. I was a terrible liar. But I didn't exactly want to admit that I'd opened up the note to read it.

'Oh?' Jack looked up at me, his brow crinkling.

'I mean, it seemed pretty awful, the stuff your dad was writing,' I said.

'It was,' Jack said with a sigh. 'I kept that so that if I needed to, I could show people what my dad was really like. That he wasn't just an old authoritarian, but that he was really fucked up in the head. I mean, who treats their family like that, Ellen?'

I shook my head, words failing me.

Just then, Jack's mobile phone, which was lying on the coffee table near mine, bleeped into life. He answered it.

'Oh hi,' he said. 'Yep, I totally understand. No, I'll come and see you, it won't be a problem at all. I'll be there in half an hour. Bye.'

As he rung off, he stood up and slipped the phone into his pocket.

I looked at him.

'Who was that?' I said.

'Oh, just DS Moretti,' Jack said, going over and grabbing his jacket from a chair. 'He wants to talk to me. Probably wants to go through the autopsy report, or something.'

'Ah, okay,' I said. But inside I was puzzled. Was that normal? It didn't sound quite right, a detective calling someone in to go through the autopsy reports of suicide. But then, what did I know? All this was new to me, I'd never had any dealing with the law before the Bryants had died, so perhaps this was perfectly standard procedure.

Jack grabbed an apple from the bowl on the counter, we said our goodbyes, and very soon he'd left the flat and was on his way to see the detective. I watched him walk past the living-room window.

I sat very still in my armchair for a while. I had a lot to process; my whole world had been turned upside down in a matter of days. Visions of the Bryants' bodies, grey and lifeless and just hanging there like dead pigs in a butchers, flashed through my mind yet again. *Did they really commit suicide?* I wondered. *Of their own accord?* That conclusion still didn't feel right to me. And I felt like my world had changed completely over the past few days. I'd slept with Jack, admitted my feelings for him while we were pissed, found him kissing Layla – although apparently that hadn't meant anything to him – and learned about his dad Dalton's toxic family abuse, and the fact that poor Penelope was probably having some sort of breakdown. Jack had told me that his dad had fallen out with a neighbour over land, and that he hadn't spoken to his elder brother for years. And I'd overheard that police officer saying that Marjorie's behaviour was unusual, that she seemed to be drawing an unusual amount of attention to herself on Saturday. And I couldn't forget Jack's callous words about his dead mother... It was clear that Dalton had upset quite a few people with his horrible attitude, and that he had many skeletons in his closet, so was it really feasible that the coroner had just decided that no foul play was involved, given the problems that surrounded the Bryants? Surely the police would at least want to investigate the situation, and interview the Bryants' neighbour who'd hated Dalton so much? What if this was his way of getting revenge on the family? Or at least they would want to contact Dalton's brother, just to take measures to ensure that nothing was overlooked? It was a lot to take in, and I couldn't quite make the simple verdict of suicide sit well, now that I had a deeper understanding of the Bryants' life.

After a while of thinking about all this, I gave myself a shake, leant forward, took a sip of tea and found that it was disgustingly cold. I put my mug down. *Right*, I thought. *I need to do something here, to put my mind at rest.* I rang the university's student office and arranged with them that I could have at least a week off my studies to process the trauma of what had happened. The woman on the other end was very nice, and said she completely understood, and that she'd be emailing me the necessary forms to fill in. I felt very grateful to her when I got off the phone. I didn't want to have to worry about work for a while, with all this going on. But what I did need to do was to lay to rest the niggling doubts at the back of my mind about what had caused the Bryant family to die in such a horrific way. *Perhaps if I go back to their house,* I thought. *I'll be able to put some of the horror in my mind to rest. Maybe I've overthought everything, as I've obviously been affected by making such a horrific discovery. I'm probably reading too much into everything; I might just need some closure. Maybe revisiting their house will help with this...*

So, knowing that Jack was safely out of the way at the police station – I didn't want him to know what I was doing, he probably wouldn't be pleased – I got my things together, and set off in the direction of the poor dead Bryant family's house...

CHAPTER TWENTY-SEVEN

W e'd had many good times there, me and Sabrina, I thought, as I walked along the pavement. Flashes of us chasing each other round the garden went through my mind, me always laughing louder and longer than she did. We played tag, we dug holes – I was obsessed with trying to dig through to Australia at one point – and we played many make-believe games out there. Sabrina was always worried about getting her clothes dirty, but I wasn't; I knew that I wouldn't get in trouble if I went home with a few grass or mud stains on me. Looking back, the poor girl must have been terrified about setting off her father's wrath. At least that's something I've never had to deal with in my own family. Sometimes, when Dalton was out or in a good mood, we would play hide-and-seek in the house. It was a good place for that; such a large building, with loads of nooks and crannies that the hider could stash themselves away in. Occasionally, when we were younger, Jack, Sam or Adele would join in with our games. Zara was just a baby then, too young to even walk, so we left her alone in Penelope's care. I remember – at one point – forming a secret society that only had us five as members. We had a secret meeting place – which was under the cherry tree at the back of their garden. Jack soon took the club over, as he said he should be in charge because he was the oldest, and I didn't mind at all, as I was totally in awe of him. No one minded that Jack liked to be in control of all the games we played. I mean, isn't that how the older kid always acts? Don't they usually like to be the boss of everything?

Those were the good, idyllic times. But there must have been bad times too. Perhaps I had blanked those out? There had clearly been something very wrong going on back then, so why was I still having such trouble defining exactly what that was? Maybe I didn't want to remember certain things that happened, even now? But why?

CHAPTER TWENTY-EIGHT

As I walked further on through the biting air, more memories of playing in that house with Sabrina when we were younger came back to me. I'd started racking my brains, trying to think of signs that I'd missed that had been screaming that all was not okay for her. Even though it upset me to spoil my view of the past, it was necessary. I owed it to Sabrina, and to Penelope, Sam, Adele and Zara. I saw now that there must have been something, some incidents in all those years, that flagged up that *something* at home that wasn't right. I may have been too ignorant and blinkered to notice the red flags then, but I was older and a bit wiser now, and I wanted to find some signs for myself that confirmed everything that Jack had recently told me about his family. It was the right thing to do, to try to piece together the bits of the puzzle. What was it that I had missed?

From what Jack had said, Dalton's behaviour towards them – especially the older two – had deteriorated as they got older, probably after they'd hit puberty and were turning from children to adults. Because he must have felt like he was losing control over them at that stage, that they were becoming too independently minded and free. When they were younger and more malleable, they'd had more freedom. They'd had friends – mainly me – over to play. Penelope hadn't looked so haggard back then. In fact, I remember thinking she was so beautiful when I was little, like Aurora's mother in Disney's *Sleeping Beauty*. So poised, so calm and collected. But when Dalton had felt his power slipping, he'd started the whole notebook thing.

But before that, when we were still at primary school, I couldn't remember things ever being too bad for Sabrina, Jack, and their younger sisters and brother. I mean, sure, they always did whatever their father said as soon as he said it. Unlike me, who would argue with my mum on occasion if she asked me to tidy up my toys if I was in the middle of a game, Sabrina and Jack were like well-trained soldiers. Dalton only had to shout for them to come in from the garden, and they would drop whatever they were doing and run straight into the house. At the time, I'd just put this down to them being perfect. Amazing looks, amazing house, amazing behaviour. But looking back, maybe it wasn't so healthy that they could never disagree with their father? Maybe it is more healthy for there to be a bit of 'safe' conflict between parents and their children?

I don't know, I'm no psychologist. I do remember one time, when Sabrina came into school really tired.

'What's wrong?' I remember asking her. 'You don't look very well?' We were about ten at the time, and getting ready to make the transition to secondary school.

'Oh, I didn't get much sleep last night,' Sabrina had said, with a big yawn. 'One of my teddies, the white sheep one, has a really fluffy, furry coat. And it started shedding white bits all over the carpet and up the stairs. My dad went mad when he saw the mess, and he made me stay up for hours, until I'd picked every single bit of white stuff out of the carpet. There were lots of them, and some of them were really stuck in, so I went to bed much later than I normally do.'

I hadn't thought much of this at the time. My mum wasn't exactly the strictest parent on earth – sometimes I thought she let me get away with answering her back a bit too much – so I just accepted that other parents disciplined their children in different ways. But looking back, why would Sabrina's dad make her lose sleep, just to pick up fluffy white bits that had fallen off a toy? It seemed a bit too much, given how young she was.

And there'd been another time, I remembered now, when I'd quietly gone back into the kitchen on my way to the toilet, needing the loo in the middle of the game we were playing. Dalton was hissing something that I couldn't hear into Penelope's ear, then he picked up a plate of food and threw the whole lot into the bin. I'd just presumed that there was something wrong with the food at the time. But looking back, there probably hadn't been. It must just have been one of his intimidation tactics, designed to make his wife feel awful. What must it have been like to be a child in a house where the dad treated the mum like that?

Memories were coming through thick and fast now. Of course, why hadn't I ever joined the dots up before? There was another time when Dalton took away all the toys in the house for a month. Sabrina told me that he said it was because he thought all the children were too spoiled, and were putting play above prayer. I do remember thinking that this was strange at the time, and feeling very sorry for Sabrina. I had loads of toys in my bedroom, and I loved playing with them in the evenings and after school. I knew that my mum would never dream of doing anything like that. But after a day or two, Sabrina's pale face went back to its normal colour, and she carried on as normal, so I didn't think anything more of it at the time, and just presumed it had happened because she had a stricter father than me.

Maybe there had been a lot of small signs – red flags – and I'd just been too young and naïve to properly pick up on them...

CHAPTER TWENTY-NINE

A s I walked along, a sudden flurry of sirens made me stop and pause for a minute. Buckingham was usually a relatively safe place, I never really felt unsafe walking around it, even in the dark. It wasn't unusual to hear the odd police car or ambulance travelling through the town, but a whole outbreak of them like the one I was listening to was unusual. I was sure that I'd hear them disappearing into the distance, like they usually did, off to one of the main roads like the A421 that lined the outskirts of the town. Unfortunately there were traffic collisions on that road from time to time, as it was very bendy, and people tried to overtake where they shouldn't. Sadly, it wasn't unknown to drive past a 'collision' sign along there every now and again, and when you saw it you hoped that it hadn't happened to anybody you knew.

But the sirens didn't go away, in fact they got louder and louder, and then stopped. It sounded like they'd come to a halt in the centre of the town. Now that was weird. Very weird.

An eerie feeling ran through me. Flashbacks of the day we'd found the Byrants' bodies flickered through my mind. Of the emergency vehicles outside, the uniformed officers, the forensic people in their suits, the paramedics, the detectives; all those professionals swarming the awful scene. That had been a one-off horrific situation, there wouldn't be another like it for centuries, I was sure of it. So many people dying in one house together was something that just didn't – shouldn't – happen in a community-minded place like Buckingham. It was outlandish, too bizarre to believe. But I had to believe it because poor Sabrina, and her five relatives, were now dead.

I saw an older lady bustling towards me. She was looking at me intently, like she wanted to talk.

Oh God, I thought. *I don't know if I'm up to a gossipy chit-chat right now.*

'Heard the sirens?' she said, an eager look on her face.

I nodded.

'My son's just phoned me,' she said, stepping closer. Suddenly she was too near to me for comfort. 'Apparently someone's been attacked in town. My son's not sure if they're alive or dead. But that's why the police and ambulances are out in force. Such a shame. Buckingham used to be a safe place to live. But what with that poor family found hanging, and now this, I'm going to make sure to lock my doors every night. And I'm not going out after dark, not until things have calmed down anyway.'

I nodded, feeling dazed all of a sudden. Someone had been attacked in town? Only a few streets away from where I stood now? This news only added to the surreal feeling that seemed to have become my normality recently. What the hell was happening to my safe little environment? I'd never worried about walking around on my own before, but all of a sudden Buckingham felt alien to me. If I'd been naïve as to what had been going on in Jack and Sabrina's family, then what else had I been missing? Had there always been a dangerous element here? I'd clearly been walking around in my own fuzzy little world for rather a long time.

I said goodbye to the woman and walked on, hoping that whoever it was that had been hurt would pull through. I'd got the feeling that she'd wanted me to stay and chat to her about the worsening state of the town for longer, but I just didn't have it in me at the moment to do that. I wanted to be alone with my thoughts while I walked. As I continued on, I tried to block out the image of yet another person getting hurt. But the sight of the bodies hanging there in the conservatory started flashing through my mind again, their faces so grey and pained. Jesus, I couldn't take much more of this...

CHAPTER THIRTY

As I approached the large property, with a biting wind whirling round me, a nausea swept through me, making me weak at the knees. The police tape was still there, flapping in the strong gusts, but this time there were no longer emergency service workers swarming around everywhere. Flashbacks of finding the Bryant family's bodies were now a constant in my mind, and my heart was pounding uncontrollably. *Oh God*, I thought. *Maybe this was a stupid idea. I should probably go home. Or maybe go and see Mum again...*

But I decided to make myself wait, and stare at the house for a bit. I was there to gain closure, I told myself. To try to move past the doubts in my mind about the suicide verdict. I mean, if professionals had decided that that was what it was, who was I to question their decision? But still...

I stared at the grey windows. The house looked dead now, too; no signs of life would be inside it for a long while. What a waste of a promising set of people, I thought, a fresh wave of sadness washing over me for their wasted lives, particularly for Sabrina and the younger children. They'd had their whole lives ahead of them, but they were all now extinguished, as though they'd never been here. It wasn't fair. For ages, everyone had thought that the Bryants were amazing; such a perfect family. How deceiving looks can be. I still couldn't get my head around it all. Maybe the house would go to Jack now? I thought. I mean, as the only surviving immediate family member, surely that's how inheritance worked? At least having that kind of security would help him process his grief. Give him somewhere stable to live, a place where he could start rebuilding his life. But was he actually grieving? I couldn't help wondering, immediately feeling guilty for having this thought. His behaviour was so erratic, so weird. But he was probably in shock, I thought. I mean, there was no right way to deal with such a tragedy, was there? It was something I found myself constantly wondering, as I'd watched his emotions flip from this way to that...

'Ellen?' a familiar voice behind me called. 'Is that you?'

I turned to see Marjorie bustling towards me, pulling her expensive-looking cardigan tightly around her generous figure. The house that she and Patrick lived in was just up the road, in the same close as the Bryants' one. They were all huge old piles round here, and must have been built at least a hundred years ago. Their gabled roofs, big stone fireplaces and old oak beams were the envy of many who lived in the smaller terraced houses at the back of the church in Buckingham town. I've always loved looking at them, and imagining what it must be like to live in them. *Shit*, I thought. *Marjorie must have seen me walk past. I'm not in the mood to talk to anyone right now, least of all Jack's aunt...*

'Hi Marjorie,' I said, walking towards her. 'How are you?'

'Devastated,' she said. And I could tell from her ashen, pained face that this was true. She looked like she'd aged ten years in a matter of days. 'What are you doing here?' Straight to the point, as usual. There was never any messing around with

Marjorie. She always cut to the chase without fluffing her words.

'I just needed some closure,' I said, struggling to find the right words to explain my presence there. 'I know this awful situation isn't nearly as bad for me as it must be for you and Jack, but I've been affected by it too, Marjorie. I keep having flashbacks, and I need to try and put them to rest. I'm finding the coroner's suicide verdict really hard to get my head around. I thought that maybe if I came back here, it might help...' I trailed off.

Marjorie stared at me. She was looking puzzled.

'Suicide verdict?' She repeated in her loud, clipped tone. 'Oh darling, you must be mistaken. The coroner didn't come to that conclusion at all. DS Moretti came to see Patrick and I yesterday, and showed us a copy of the report. The result was an open verdict, or conclusion as they now call it. The police and the coroner all believe that the deaths are suspicious, but as yet they don't have the evidence to reach any other decision.'

CHAPTER THIRTY-ONE

I stared at Marjorie, my mouth hanging open. I couldn't believe what I was hearing.

'But Jack said–' I began.

'Ah yes, Jack,' she said, cutting across my words. 'I think you and I need to have a chat, Ellen. Come back to my house, and I'll make us some tea. There are some things I probably need to tell you.'

Several minutes later, I found myself sitting opposite Jack's aunt, at her solid oak dining table. *Should I be worried about being here?* I wondered, watching her pour the tea. We'd walked past her husband Patrick on the way in. He'd been firmly ensconced in an armchair, and had been reading *The Telegraph*. I very much doubted whether he would come and join us, as he tended to be a man of few words. His wife more than made up for that. She generally dominated the discussion whenever the two of them were present, and I could see that today was going to be no exception.

I was remembering the police officer's comment about Marjorie's behaviour seeming suspicious. I tried to listen to my gut instinct, to see if it was telling me anything. Did she know more about the deaths than she was letting on? Could she even be involved somehow? But everything felt okay, there was nothing that was making me feel unsafe or in danger. When she'd turned up at the Bryants' house on Saturday, calling for Penelope, her behaviour hadn't seemed that strange to me, because I was used to her. I'd known her for years, through Sabrina. And if I'm honest, she'd always been a busybody; one to try to take charge of any situation. *At the very least, I should stay and talk to the woman,* I decided. She'd just thrown a clanger of a curveball at me about the coroner's report, and my head was in a whirl. If she could shed any light on this confusing situation, and help me understand just what the fuck was going on with Jack, then having a chat with her would be worth it...

'So,' Marjorie said, pushing a small porcelain teacup towards me. 'It's time that we discussed my nephew, isn't it?'

I nodded. All I could think was: *Why did Jack lie to me? Why the hell would he not tell me the truth about something so important? How could he think that I wouldn't find out the truth?*

Before we'd sat down, Marjorie had collected some papers from a desk drawer. She stared at them for a minute, then pushed them over towards me.

I looked down and started to read the first document.

Autopsy authorised by Dr David Walker. Deceased: Penelope Bryant

Oh God, I stopped reading for a minute and closed my eyes. This was all too awful. It made it all the more real, seeing Penelope's name down on paper like that. But I had to know the truth. I forced myself to open my eyes and keep reading.

Undernourished white female… Urgh, I couldn't make myself read all the details. I quickly scanned down the page to the bottom. *Cause of death: Open conclusion.*

I stared up at Marjorie, crazy thoughts going round in my head. Could she have faked this report? Could this all be another lie? I no longer knew who to trust. But she had tears in her eyes. I felt she was sincere in her grief. I looked down and reread the line again.

Open conclusion.

'I'm so sorry for your loss,' I said, barely able to get my words out. 'I'm feeling so confused, Marjorie. Jack told me – clear as day – that the autopsy report had ruled all the deaths as suicide. We talked about it for ages afterwards. He was so convincing, and I didn't think for a moment that he wasn't telling the truth. Why would he lie to me about that?'

Marjorie sighed, and wiped a tear from her cheek.

'Patrick and I have only realised how much Jack takes after his father, Dalton, over the last year,' she said, her expression very serious. 'Before that, we felt as sorry for him as we did for the rest of the family. But he's been showing more and more signs of being obsessed with control and power, which – unfortunately – my brother always liked, too. As poor Penelope and the children found out. Has Jack told you anything about what went on behind closed doors as he was growing up?'

'Yes,' I said. I told Marjorie everything that Jack had divulged about his father, including what I knew about the notebooks, the control and the abuse. I explained that Jack had told me about his father's cruelty towards him and his siblings, how he treated them when they were younger, and how he said that God was talking to him, telling him messages that he needed to pass on to his family members. I didn't tell her about the notebook page that had fallen out of Jack's coat pocket though, the one I'd picked up and read. Marjorie didn't need to know about that for now, and I didn't want her to think that I'd been sneaking or prying. Knowing something like that might potentially stop her from opening up to me.

Jack's aunt sat quietly, listening to what I had to say, nodding her head every now and again.

'That's all true,' she said when I'd finished. 'Unfortunately my brother decided to emulate our own father's behaviour. He would do a similar thing, you see; write down instructions for my mother in a grotty little book, ordering her to work harder, and criticising her for being a lazy wife. It was awful, growing up in that household.'

I nodded, remembering how Jack had told me about that too.

'My brother, Dalton, chose to take matters even further,' Marjorie said, pain washing over her face. 'I'm not quite sure why, as he must have remembered how awful it was to be a child growing up in such an environment. He and I hated living in our family house, constantly seeing our mother in tears with our father berating her. In my heart, I know it's why our brother Jacob moved away. Perhaps he saw too much of my father in him, and wanted a clean break. I know that he and Dalton fell out over money, and being the dutiful sister that I was, I took Dalton's side, as I've always been much closer to him than to Jacob. Although I realise now that that might have been a mistake.' She paused. 'My father's behaviour towards my mother is one of the reasons that Patrick and I decided to never start a family,' she went on. 'I couldn't bear the idea of bringing children into this world, in case I turned out to be a parent like my father was to me, or a weak, broken one like my mother. I never wanted to subject any children of my own to even a slice of what I had to put up with, growing up. It's made me the woman I am today, but unfortunately it also made Dalton into the tyrant that he became. That sort of thing can push you one way or another, Ellen.'

She paused, looking away for a moment. I sat still and waited for her to continue.

'When Dalton's children were much younger,' she went on, 'particularly when they only had Jack and Sabrina, things were much better in that household. Dalton was always strict with them, and always made sure they studied the bible and went to church every Sunday, but they had a better life. The children were allowed to have fun and see friends. People were invited back to their house, and the atmosphere there was controlled, but happier. Penelope was more together then, too. I remember the wonderful cakes and pastries she would bake; their kitchen always smelt of her delicious cooking. She would take great delight in choosing clothes for the children – Dalton wanted everyone to look smart and well-dressed all the time – and of course, they could afford it. That's when she had at least some access to their finances.'

I nodded, remembering how I used to go on play dates with Sabrina, and how I desperately wanted to be sucked into the Bryant family, and become one of them. They'd seemed like golden people to me back then. I'd even fantasised about Penelope and Dalton adopting me at one point. How I wanted to look as smart and beautiful as Sabrina, and have polished manners like Sam, and my hair done perfectly like Adele. How I'd wanted to eat their meals, sleep in their perfect beds, and have Penelope fluttering around in the kitchen looking after me. But how glad was I now, that that was never a real possibility?

'I think Dalton and Penelope went on to have too many children,' Marjorie said. 'My brother used to despair about what would become of them in this "evil world", as he called it. He was so worried that they would be sucked into the vices of life, such as drink, drugs or gambling, and turn their back on the Lord. We've always been a devoutly religious clan,' she said, almost defiantly. 'God has guided us throughout our lives. But something went wrong; Dalton's thinking went awry. I think this was caused out of worry for his children. In the end, nothing was good enough for him; Penelope got the brunt of his anger, poor woman. But the older two children also felt the power of his control, even more than the other three, in my opinion. I think there were just too many children for my brother to sanely cope with in the end. He felt that he needed to have total control over all of them, but it was – as they say – like herding cats. How can one have complete control over five growing children? It's impossible, at least, it is without using very extreme measures. When Sabrina confided in me about the notebooks her father was writing one day, I could hardly bear it–' Marjorie broke off. I watched as another tear rolled down her cheek.

'I couldn't believe that my brother was replicating the pain that he and I had lived through as children. It was all so unnecessary,' she said. 'I genuinely believe he thought that by writing down the word of God – as he saw it – to influence the behaviour of his family, he was helping to protect them from falling off the righteous path. But he went too far, and in the end he was actually harming them, rather than helping them.'

'I think so too,' I said. 'It sounds as though Dalton's behaviour had become quite abusive, Marjorie.'

She gave me a piercing look. Then her shoulders sagged.

'Yes, I know that you're right,' she said. 'Abuse is a good word for it. It's just so hard for me to admit the depths to which my brother had sunk. You see, I loved him so much, Ellen. After we'd fallen out with our brother Jacob, Dalton and I became very close. If I'm honest, I know that I should have done more to curb his behaviour towards Penelope and the children. I did try and talk to him about it one day, but he got so angry that I had to stop. I decided then to step back from the situation and to not interfere, with the hope that once the children had grown up, they could move away from the family house and start their own lives. Like I had done, when I was younger. I couldn't bear the thought of losing him as a brother too. His anger had shown me that this would be a real possibility, and I just couldn't go through with alienating him.'

I felt an anger rising in me when she said this. To know that she could have done more to stop Jack's father's abuse, but that she'd chosen not to, due to some misplaced loyalty towards her brother, was a hard pill to swallow. She'd made a selfish decision with that. If an intervention had taken place earlier, Penelope and Jack's siblings could well be alive today. Maybe social services could have got involved. Perhaps the children could have gone to live in foster homes, or anywhere away from Dalton's obsessive control. Their schools would no doubt have been told, and the teachers would have kept a closer eye on them. My mum would probably have found out somehow – parents always did – and she might have helped me to help them. It seemed like such a missed opportunity. But I didn't want to let my bile show, because I was learning so much from Marjorie, and I knew that there was more to come. She was opening up wonderfully, and I wanted her to continue. I was still in the dark about Jack, and his motives for lying to me. So I just nodded, and waited for her to carry on talking, biting down my true feelings.

'This is very hard for me,' Marjorie said. 'Sharing the problems in my family with you like this. You see, we were brought up to keep everything "in house", if you understand what I mean. We were told never to air our dirty laundry in public, but to keep all problems firmly behind closed doors. I'm not at all used to opening up to people outside the family in this way, Ellen.'

'I do understand,' I said, nodding. 'But the thing is, Marjorie, events have turned too serious to keep things secret anymore. Six people are dead – hung in the most awful of circumstances – six of your relatives, and Jack is acting really strangely. If you know anything, anything at all that might help me understand Jack's weird behaviour, then I would be really grateful if you could share it with me. Because at the moment, I feel like I'm going mad. And I'm worried that Jack is going crazy too. I don't understand what happened to his family, or why, and I don't understand why my so-called best friend would lie to me about the coroner's verdict.'

This time it was my turn to have tears in my eyes. The betrayal at finding out Jack had been dishonest about such an important thing stung so much that I was in physical pain. I just wanted answers, reasons for the way he was acting. That would explain away his weird choices and behaviour. I so wanted to still believe in my friend, to feel that he was a good person. But the foundations of my trust in him had been severely shaken, and it made my heart feel like it was plummeting downwards towards Marjorie's parquet flooring.

'Yes, yes. You're right.' Marjorie gazed at me. 'It's time for me to tell you a few home truths about Jack. For your own sake as much as anything else.'

CHAPTER THIRTY-TWO

Marjorie had been an ever-present figure in the Bryants' lives for as long as I'd known them. Her voice booming in the kitchen, her phone calls to Dalton, her turning up unexpectedly at the house every so often, her reprimands and religious warnings, the boring presents she gave my friends at Christmas, like the tweed skirt thirteen-year-old Sabrina received – which I don't believe she wore once – and the book on etiquette that she gave Jack. I doubt he ever read it.

I never warmed to Marjorie; she'd always seemed like a caricature of herself, too upright, too well-behaved to be true. Almost like a prop in a play; a background fixture that doesn't ever offer much true feeling or value. But the woman visibly crumbling before me was a very different person. I could suddenly see the humanity in her, as her scales of social conditioning fell away. *Oh God,* I thought. *Who out of the Bryant clan was real? Were there any of them that hadn't been putting on some act or other over the years?* Images of my own flawed but real family members flashed through my head, and I was instantly grateful for each one of them, and remorseful that

I'd ever wanted to belong to a different family. That I'd idolised the bloody Bryants. My brother Tom was an angry young man, but he never pretended to be anything other than who he was. Before he'd been sent away to his boarding school, he'd got into fights, sworn at teachers and been really vile to me and Mum. He wore his emotions on his sleeve, and I always knew where I was with him; which was usually on the receiving end of some bruise or other. Mum had gone through stages of being an emotional wreck, but again she lived honestly about that, never pretended that she was okay when she wasn't. Sobbing when she needed to, talking to her friends about how she was feeling for hours on the phone, and searching for local counsellors on the internet. And as irritating as I'd found her 'weakness', I suddenly perceived it as strength. She'd had the guts to admit that she was falling apart, and had been able to slowly work her way through it. Even Dad had never covered up the fact that he was an unfaithful dick to Mum. He'd fessed up everything to me after he'd left, hanging his head in shame. My family members now seemed so real and actualised compared to the Bryants, who had apparently been acting in some sort of social play of their own devising. They'd been doing all the right things outwardly, and had fooled myself and many others into thinking they were fine upstanding members of the community; a model family. They'd certainly pulled the wool over my eyes, and for my part I'd gladly let them. But it had all been a show. They weren't like that in reality. But they'd never let the outside world see the sordidness that had gone on inside their house. The abuse, the pain, the domination, the control, the punishments, the 'notebooks from God'. It was cowardly; all unreal. What the hell had Dalton been thinking?

Marjorie's shoulders were sagging, and all of a sudden she looked like a tired old lady, rather than the grand stately woman that she usually appeared to be. *What on earth could she be about to tell me?* I wondered. *What more was there to know about Jack and his broken family?*

CHAPTER THIRTY-THREE

I sat up a bit, and waited.

'Like I was saying before,' Marjorie said, her voice no longer the confident boom that it usually was. 'We've only realised recently how much like his father – Dalton – Jack is. And that's not a very good thing, because he seems to have inherited the male Bryant obsession with power, money and control. My father had it, my brother had it, and now Jack seems to be following in their footsteps.'

She bent her head down for a moment. I felt a pang of sympathy for her; I could tell how hard this was for her to say. But still, it was something I needed to know.

'For a while, Penelope seemed so much brighter after my brother passed away,' Marjorie said, looking up again. 'And who could blame her? Dalton had acted like a tyrant, and made her life hell. Written down instructions to keep her and the children at heel. When he'd gone, she must have started feeling like she had a new lease of life. The colour gradually came back into her cheeks, she started eating more – she'd become stick thin previously – and the worry lines on her face began to relax. She started wearing her nice clothes again. Did you see much of her at this stage, over the last few years?'

I shook my head.

'No,' I said. 'As we got older, I tended to meet up with Jack, and sometimes Sabrina, outside their house. I didn't notice it so much at the time, but I think they'd made a decision to stop inviting me round so much. Maybe they didn't want me to see their mum deteriorating. We did pop round now and again, and I had noticed the amount of weight that Penelope had lost. But to be honest I put it down to her grief at losing her husband, the stress of being a single mother to five, and the fact that she was getting older.'

Marjorie nodded.

'And you weren't a mind reader, Ellen, so you must never blame yourself for not spotting what was going on in that house. Even I barely knew for a long while. Anyway, when Penelope started looking better and more healthy, both Patrick and I were very much encouraged and pleased by this turn of events. I've never been close to Penelope – Dalton made sure of that – but anyone who put up with my brother's bullish behaviour for as long as she did, earns my respect. And the simple fact is, that I wanted her to be happy. Because the more content she was, the more the children would thrive.'

I nodded, agreeing with this sentiment. Happy mother, happy children.

'But about six months after Dalton died,' Marjorie went on, 'Penelope's newly acquired glow began to fade. She stopped smiling, the colour drained from her face, and she stopped going out. She lost even more weight than before, and was a rack of bones by the end. It was perplexing, and to start with I was worried that she'd fallen ill. That was until poor Sabrina came round to see me one day, absolutely distraught.'

I sat up a bit straighter, eager to hear what she was going to say next.

'Sabrina told me that Jack had started behaving like Dalton had at home. That he was fine for the first few months after his dad had passed, but that one day he started behaving like a man possessed. He announced to the family that he was now the head of them, and that his word would now be law in that house. That he expected them to do as he said.'

'Really?' I said, exhaling. I was trying to fit this information into the mental map I had of who Jack was. A few days ago, I wouldn't have believed a word of it. But now, it didn't seem completely ludicrous. And that was sad. 'So it was Jack who was stressing his mum out after his dad died?'

'Sadly, yes,' Marjorie said. 'I couldn't console Sabrina, she was so upset. She told me that Jack had started writing instructions for them in the notebooks, picking up where Dalton had left off. But his line was that he was channelling his dead father's words. He said that Dalton was now with God in heaven, and that from now on he would be directing the Divine word to Jack, who would impart it to the rest of the family. She said that Jack had become unbearably cruel, especially towards the younger ones, and that he was also being awful to the neighbour's cat, throwing it over the fence as hard as he could whenever he got the opportunity. She also told me that Jack was constantly badgering their mother for money, and was trying to force her to release his inheritance to him early. Dalton left Penelope with a hefty pile of money, but with strict instructions in the will to be frugal, and not to spoil the children with it. It was too much for Sabrina to cope with. She'd been enjoying her freedom since her father died, and couldn't bear to go back to being so controlled. And her mother – the desperate, broken woman – was so trained to follow male instructions, that she just gave in to Jack. Did nothing to protect the rest of the children. Perhaps she couldn't. Maybe that sort of thing was beyond her capabilities by then. I bumped into her once in the street, and for a moment it seemed as though she wanted to tell me something. I waited with her for a while, but in the end she just shook her head and walked off. I mean, we both knew that Jack hadn't had an easy time of it when he was little. That he'd got the brunt of my brother's anger. Dalton used to lock him in the dark cellar when he was naughty, and I think that experience changed Jack. So Penelope – and I for that matter – have always felt rather protective over him.'

'So what did you do?' I said. 'When Sabrina told you what Jack was doing?'

'I told her not to worry, and to leave the information with me,' Marjorie said. 'I told her that Jack was probably just going through a phase, and that it would wear off soon. I told her not to take any notice of him.'

I fought the urge to roll my eyes. Why had Marjorie not done more? She'd known about what was going on in that house, and yet again had done nothing. She hadn't alerted the authorities, she'd made no report. None of the younger children's schools were any the wiser that this was happening, so the whole lot of them had to go into a second phase of suffering and oppression. Apparently at the hands of my 'best friend'. It was too much.

'But when Sabrina came to see me a couple of days later, and told me that Jack was stopping his mother from eating meals as a punishment for not getting all of the chores done on time,' Marjorie went on, 'I decided that enough was enough. I'd always been a bit scared of Dalton. But I wasn't frightened of my nephew Jack one bit. We'd been raised never to involve the authorities in our private lives. But Jack is a lot younger than me, and if anything, he should be showing his elders some respect, not the other way around. If Penelope was having her food restricted, I knew that they needed outside help. So I phoned the police.'

'Oh.' I was surprised. 'Well that's good. What did they do?'

'They came round and spoke to the family,' Marjorie said. 'Sabrina was more than willing to talk to them, from what she told me afterwards. But Penelope just clammed up. Wouldn't say anything, and definitely wouldn't press charges. So apart from warning Jack to leave his mother and siblings alone, there wasn't much that the police could do. I believe he asked you if he could move into your flat not long after this incident.'

I stared at the woman opposite me. I wanted so badly not to believe a word of what she was saying, to instead suspect that she was the bad one. But my gut feeling told me that she was telling the truth. A fresh wave of sadness went through me, as I remembered how Jack had said that he'd decided to ask me if he could move into my spare room because the atmosphere in the house was too awful for him to cope with, even after Dalton had died. That he wanted a fresh start, someplace where he could heal and find himself again. But if what Marjorie said was true, then these words of Jack's were more bullshit. He hadn't moved out because he was depressed and needed to heal, he'd moved out because his awful behaviour had been reported to the police by his aunt. Why the hell was Marjorie only telling me this now? I wondered. A bit of a heads-up at the time would have been nice. But maybe she was doing what she'd always done, keeping news about his behaviour 'in house'. I wasn't sure I could listen to her talking any more that day, as my brain was already overflowing with information that needed processing. And I felt cut up emotionally. Now I was the one who definitely needed time to heal.

'Thank you so much for telling me all this Marjorie,' I said, standing up. 'I need to be getting back now, but it would be great to chat more to you in the future.'

Marjorie tore a strip of paper off one of the photocopies on the table and scribbled down a number on it, then gave it to me.

'There's still more that I need to tell you,' she said. 'Perhaps we can meet again soon. Here, take my number. Phone me if you ever need to. And Ellen?'

'Yes?' I said, walking towards the door, while stuffing her number into my jacket pocket.

'Be very careful,' she said.

I walked as fast as I could back to my flat. As I passed a house, I saw a newspaper lying on the doorstep. *Open Conclusion Recorded for the Six Hanging Bodies*, I read. I walked on, I couldn't bear to read any more. Jesus, why the fuck did Jack lie to me about that? It seemed so stupid. Surely he must have known that I would soon find out the truth, I mean, it wasn't exactly a secret, was it? Maybe he was going mad. Perhaps the stress of everything that had happened had got to him more than I'd realised. But still, the things that Marjorie had told me about him were sick, so worrying. I felt like *I* was the one going mad, I didn't know what or who to believe anymore.

I didn't let myself go until the front door was firmly shut behind me. Then the huge, racking sobs that had been wanting to surface ever since I found out what a liar Jack was exploded out of me. I slid down on to the carpet, and cried and cried. There was a physical pain in my heart. Because it turned out that I didn't know the man who I thought I loved at all. If what Marjorie said was true – and deep down I knew that it was – Jack wasn't a nice person. He was a fraudster. He pretended to be something that he wasn't. And stupid, stupid me had fallen for him; what a dumb idiot. If he'd lied about the autopsy results to me, what else had he said that wasn't true? How could any of this be happening? A fresh wave of sobbing overtook me.

Just then, I heard a key being inserted into the lock of the front door. It was Jack. The lying bastard was home. What the fuck should I do?

CHAPTER THIRTY-FOUR

As Jack walked through the front door, he saw me sobbing and smiled his cheeky grin at me. My despair turned to anger.

'What the fuck have you been playing at?' I said, my voice getting louder with each word. I stood up and faced him. 'You lying bastard. Did you think I wouldn't find out the truth about the autopsies? That I'm so stupid and gullible that you can tell me anything and I'll just take your word for it? Jesus, Jack. Who the fuck actually are you? I feel like I don't know you at all.'

'Woah.' Jack put both his hands out in a placating way. His happy expression had turned into a concerned one. 'Are you okay, Ellen? I've been a bit worried about you over the last few days, if I'm honest. I think seeing what we did on Saturday has really affected you. Do you think you might need medical help? God bless you.'

'Just shut the fuck up,' I said loudly between sobs. 'Don't you dare "bless me". Stop playing the fucking fool with me, Jack. I've just been talking to your aunt, Marjorie. And she'd told me a few hard facts about you. Like the fact that you lied to me about the autopsy results. They're not recorded as suicides, they're open conclusions, as you well know. And she told me about how you started controlling your mother and siblings after Dalton died. You're not a nice person, Jack, so stop pretending to be.'

I turned and walked off into my bedroom, slamming the door hard behind me. How could I have been so stupid? Why didn't I see any of this? My Jack, my wonderful Jack – who I'd been thinking about morning, noon and night for so long – was actually an arsehole. The memory about him that had been trying to come through was getting closer to being in my consciousness. Yes, that's right, Jack had done something when all of us kids were playing together in the garden together one day...

'Ellen?' Jack was calling through the door. He sounded upset. 'Ellen, can I come in? I think I've got some explaining to do.'

'No,' I shouted back. 'Go away. I don't want to hear any more bullshit come out of your mouth, Jack.'

There was a rustle of papers outside my door.

'I think you're going to want to hear what I have to say, Ellen,' Jack said. 'And I've got proof to back it up, right here in my hands. I'm not the liar, Ellen, my Aunt Marjorie is. And I've got the evidence to show you exactly why right here. I've had it in my room, ready and waiting, in case things ever came to this.'

CHAPTER THIRTY-FIVE

I didn't want to open that door. Something inside me was warning me against it, telling me not to engage with any more of Jack's lies and bullshit. But then another part of me, hearing the angst in his voice, remembered my love for this man. I wasn't sure that I did still love him – not in the pure way that I had been anyway. Everything was fucked up now; complicated. I knew I couldn't trust him; I didn't know who the real Jack was anymore. I felt like I was going mad. But I was wondering what documents he could possibly have that would refute Marjorie's words? I remembered the tears in his aunt's eyes, how genuinely sad and grief-stricken she'd seemed as we discussed his family.

In one impulsive movement, I opened my bedroom door, snatched the pile of papers from Jack's hands, tried not to notice the pleading look on his face, then slammed the door shut again. I walked over to my bed, sat down, and began to read.

My client, Marjorie Hall, has reasonable grounds with which to contest the will of her late brother, Dalton Bryant, I read. *I am therefore submitting an Inheritance Act claim on her behalf.*

I lowered the papers. *Really?* I thought. *Why the hell had Marjorie not mentioned this when we were speaking earlier.*

There was knocking on my bedroom door.

'Ellen?' Jack called. 'Can I come in? I can talk you through the papers. There's a lot of them, and the legal language is complicated in parts. If you let me come in I can guide you through it all.'

'No,' I said loudly. 'Go away. I don't want to talk to you at the moment, Jack. Just leave me alone.'

There was a pause.

'Fine,' Jack called back, his tone low and dejected. 'I'll go out for a bit and give you some space.' I knew he hated any type of rejection, that it was definitely one of his triggers, but for once his feelings weren't at the top of my list of things to worry about.

Seconds later, I heard the front door open, then shut. Silence.

I picked up the papers again, and tried to concentrate on more of their contents, but my brain was all over the place; my thoughts whirling. So much had happened, I was finding it hard to process. I looked down the page. Phrases such as: `Invalid`, `entitled to more of her brother's estate`, and `earlier will`, caught my attention.

Christ, this was too much. There was no way I could take in all this information. But I didn't want Jack next to me either, breathing down my neck, and potentially filling my head with more untruths. There was only one way to find out what the fuck was going on. My hand went to my jacket pocket – I still hadn't taken it off since arriving back at the flat – and pulled out the piece of paper with Marjorie's number on it. Confronting the woman with this new information was the only way forward. I wanted to hear what she had to say for herself.

CHAPTER THIRTY-SIX

'Marjorie?' I was aware that I barked her name like a sergeant major when she answered the phone, but I was past caring.

'Yes?' she said.

'This is Ellen,' I said. 'Listen, Jack's just given me a whole bunch of papers about something that you never mentioned to me when we were chatting earlier. I wanted to get your perspective on it, as I now don't know what to think.'

'Right,' Marjorie said. She didn't sound surprised.

'The documents are about you contesting Dalton's will,' I went on. 'From what I can see, you're making a claim on the grounds that you don't think you inherited enough from Dalton's estate when he died.'

There was a sigh.

'Well I did tell you that I had more to explain to you, didn't I?' Marjorie said. 'But you seemed so keen to rush off before I had the chance, Ellen. Yes, Patrick and I decided that it was the right thing to do to challenge the will. But for very good reasons. I'm not just a greedy old woman who wanted to take money away from my sister-in-law and nieces and nephews, you know.

Believe it or not, I care very much about all of them. No, the problem that I could see developing – after my brother died – was actually one caused by Jack. Sabrina told me – on several occasions – about how much pressure he was putting on their mother to sign over his share of his inheritance early. He's always been a lazy boy, hardly worked at all in school, despite his bright brain. Now he says he's a writer. But where's all his work? What's he actually written? Nothing ever seems to come of it, he's all talk and no do. In my opinion, Jack wanted an easy future, funded by getting his inheritance early. And with everything else that was going on in the house, I could tell that Penelope was seriously at breaking point. I actually spoke to her about contesting the will, and she agreed that it would be a good idea. Because if she didn't legally have the money to give to Jack, then no matter how much he bullied her about it, there would be no way she could sign it over to him. I think she was hoping that he'd pull himself together, and finally get a job of some sort. The idea was going to be, that if I was legally awarded a larger part of the inheritance, then I would make a new will that divided it up to all of Penelope's children at the time of my death. So everything would be fair and square. You see, in the end, we'd both become concerned that even if she did give Jack an early inheritance, his demands wouldn't stop there. He would want more and more, until he had drained her dry. This seemed the logical, legal way of getting round his avarice.'

I was quiet, absorbing her words.

'Oh I see,' I said eventually. 'Do you have any proof of this? That Penelope was in agreement with you about the will?'

'Yes,' Marjorie said. 'She'd had a lawyer confirm that she was happy to proceed in this way. We simply had to go through the legalities of me contesting the will, to make it all right, so that the money would be untouchable by Jack until my death. I can show you everything that I have about it, the next time you visit. I was running along quite smoothly in that department, and was nearly at completion. But then they all died.'

'Christ,' I whispered. Should I trust what she was saying? I wondered. God, I didn't know who was telling the truth anymore.

'Jack was upset that I'd been speaking to you,' I said, my voice a mumble now.

'You told him?' Marjorie's tone was rising now. 'Why did you tell him you'd spoken to me? Oh, you silly girl. Have you still really got no idea of what that boy is actually like?'

'Sorry,' I whispered.

'No, don't be sorry,' Marjorie said. 'Just get yourself out of your flat for a while, Ellen. Go and stay somewhere that Jack is unfamiliar with. I can't emphasise the importance of this enough, and I've told DS Moretti all my suspicions about my nephew. He said that they are watching him, too, but at the moment they don't have enough evidence to make an arrest. I hate saying this, and I wish things were different, but the simple fact is that you must keep yourself safe from Jack, my dear. God knows what he is capable of. I can now see that I should have spoken to you before, that I should have warned you about my nephew at an earlier date. But you see, I just couldn't. I've been in denial about what Jack's really like for a long time. I wanted my family to be a close, upstanding one for so long, Ellen. And for society to view us in that way too. I fooled myself about it, and overlooked things that I shouldn't have. Spent too long trying to preserve a fantasy that just doesn't exist. For everything to be all right, when it wasn't. I understand that now. And it's time for me to speak up, and to warn you of how important it is that you look after yourself. And although I say this with a heavy heart, I must compel you to do your utmost to protect yourself from my nephew.'

CHAPTER THIRTY-SEVEN

I laid the phone down next to me on the bed, and stared into space for several minutes. Could this really be happening? I wondered. My beloved Jack was actually a dangerous person who I had to keep myself safe from? I felt like I'd fallen down a rabbit hole into some surreal land. But unlike Alice in Wonderland, my new world wasn't fun and full of talking animals. It was like a horror movie. My trust in everything I knew was being severely shaken and I hated it. The worst thing was that I knew I wasn't going to just wake up, and shake the experience off. This was real. It was all really happening. But how could it be?

A large part of me wanted Jack to come back to the flat and give me a really reasonable, believable explanation that combatted everything his aunt had said. I just didn't want to give up my feelings for him. They were everything to me, I'd built my life around them. Sad as that may sound, it was true. I thought about Jack from the moment I woke up in the morning, to the moment I fell asleep, and sometimes I even dreamed about him too. If I had to accept that he wasn't who I thought he was, if he wasn't my beloved, magnetic Jack Bryant who had wowed me ever since I'd seen him up that tree that time, then where did that leave me?

I could feel my thoughts, my sense of self, crashing around me. I didn't know who I was anymore. Why the hell had I allowed myself to get lost in my imagined sense of who Jack was? Of what his whole family were like? I'd been so blind, so wilfully stupid, for so many years. Marjorie's words just wouldn't get out of my head. *Get yourself out of your flat for a while*, she'd said. She'd also told me that she'd discussed Jack with DS Moretti. She clearly thought he had something to do with his family's murders. She didn't trust her own nephew, and this was coming from a woman to whom family meant everything. Who'd kept terrible family secrets because she'd been brought up to keep everything 'in house'. If she was so certain and was now prepared to break her family's code of honour, then maybe I needed to take her words seriously...

CHAPTER THIRTY-EIGHT

I was in a daze as I stuffed a few possessions into a bag. Underwear, a change of clothes, phone charger, laptop. God knows what else I'd need. I knew where I was heading. My mum's house. Yes, Jack knew where it was, but I couldn't honestly believe he would try anything with me being there. The concept of him harming me at all was very unreal. Alien to me. I mean, this was the man who I'd been madly in love with for so long. And until today, I had believed was a good, but complicated person. Now everything I'd known had been blown apart. And I needed my mum. I needed her comforting arms around me. And I wanted to get away from the flat, and from Jack, indefinitely. Until my head felt better, and till I knew what the fuck was going on.

I had no idea if I had everything that I needed, as I closed my front door behind me, and set off in the direction of my mum's house. I peered up and down the pavement, wondering where Jack had gone. I didn't want him to see me leaving, or to ask any questions. I just wanted to be with my mum and brother right now, and to be left alone.

Pulling my hood up to block out the cold drizzle that was

falling on me, I decided to take the short cut to Mum's. I wanted to get there as quickly as I could, and the weather was shit and I was already shivering. So I turned off the main road and down one of the alleys that only the locals used. They criss-crossed down the backs of many of the older residential areas around Buckingham, and were often used as shortcuts. They were a handy way of getting to the park, and to the play area at the top of town. Teenagers used them to smoke in, too. And they were often a haunt of dog walkers. I used them quite frequently myself, especially if I was running late for something. I didn't think twice about turning off the pavement and into the mouth of the nearest alley...

Good, I thought. There was no one around. Suited me perfectly, I wasn't in the mood for social interaction. There was no way I wanted to politely smile at someone, or nod my head in a greeting. I just wasn't in the mood.

I'd only been walking a few minutes, when a sudden thump on the back of my head caused me to crumple. Horrific pain. Everything went black.

CHAPTER THIRTY-NINE

'Where am I?' I couldn't get the words out. There was some sort of material gagging my mouth. For a moment or two, I was stuck in the liminal space between consciousness and unconsciousness. Nothing felt real, and I had no idea where I was.

But then the cold kicked in. Not just cold, utter arctic freezing. I realised that my whole body was shaking. And that my hands were bound above my head. And that I was wet. And it smelled of rotting dampness. Fuck, it was like I'd woken up in hell.

Why was I wet? I opened my eyes and looked around. At first, everything seemed pitch black. But as my sight adjusted to the hellhole that I found myself in, I started to make out certain things. Glimmers of dull light were shining down from above me, and I could tell that I was in a small space. It felt like I was outside in the cold air, but inside somewhere at the same time. I moved my feet a bit as it suddenly dawned on me that my legs – as well as my arms – were in a lot of aching pain. My right foot slipped off whatever I was standing on, and for a minute seemed to be suspended in the air, with nothing underneath it. Shit.

Fuck. A whoosh of extreme fear ran through me, and I quickly moved my foot backwards on to solid ground. Was I standing on a ledge of some sort? And more to the point, was I alone? Was my captor hiding somewhere?

My aching brain – it felt like it had been run over – tried to work out the sequence of events that had led to me being in this horrendous, bitterly glacial, stinking place. I'd been to see Marjorie, I could remember that. Then I'd gone home and Jack had arrived. As soon as I thought of him, my fear levels increased. Jack. He wasn't a good person. Ah yes, I thought. That's right, I'd decided to go and see my mum; I'd wanted a break from the real world, and for her to look after me for a while. So I'd set off across Buckingham to her house. I'd decided to take the shortcut, as it was quicker. Then a pain at the back of my head, then blackness. The last thing I could remember was walking down that alley...

Whichever way I looked at it, the only logical conclusion seemed to be that someone had attacked me, knocked me out, then taken me to whatever shit pit I was in right now. It all seemed so surreal. Surely this kind of thing only happened in movies? But no, the pain in my arms – stretched high above my head – was too tangibly awful for me to be dreaming all this. But who had done this to me? I was very afraid that I already knew the answer to this question. I didn't want it to be him, but who else could it be? Marjorie?

Memories of the last few days floated back through my head. Experiencing them was like a waking nightmare. I'd found the six Bryant bodies hanging from their conservatory roof on Saturday morning. Jack had been there too. It had been a sickeningly horrific sight. The police hadn't been sure whether they'd committed suicide or been murdered. The coroner had recorded an open conclusion, although Jack had lied and said it was suicide. Marjorie had evidence that Jack was a liar. Jack had evidence that Marjorie was contesting his dad's will. Dalton had been an evil tyrant. Everything was so fucked up. And now I was half hanging, half standing, in near darkness, in a place that felt like a well. Or maybe – from the stench of it – a sewer. It didn't take a genius to work out that it was probably the person who'd had something to do with the Bryants' deaths who'd done this to me. And I had to believe that that person was my former best friend and the man I'd been in love with for years. Jack.

But, my brain quickly countered, could I be really sure of that? I mean, Dalton had offended many people. His neighbour was apparently furious with him over the dispute about land. His sister Marjorie was contesting his will; she said it was for very good reasons, but could I believe her? Even his brother Jacob, who he hadn't spoken to for years, could hate him, although why I wasn't sure. Perhaps he'd found some reason to exact revenge on his brother's family? Dalton had clearly been a beast in human form, and like the rest of his family, had pretended to the outside world that he was a fine, upstanding, churchgoing citizen. Well, if I survived this experience, I knew one thing for sure – I'd never judge people on how they superficially presented themselves to the world. I'd look deep, so deep into them that I could see into their souls, before awarding them even an ounce of my trust.

There was a noise above me. The stony grating noise indicated that a heavy slab was being pulled away. I tried to look up, an icy chill shooting through my veins. Grey daylight suddenly illuminated the space I was in, and I could see the slimy wall in front of me, not three feet away from my face, that was covered in thick moss and lichen. I seemed to be in a well. It looked like an old space, something that had existed for years.

'Ah, hello Ellen,' Jack's voice said. He sounded cheery. 'I see you've woken up.'

CHAPTER FORTY

A nger immediately overtook the fear I'd been feeling. I could feel it warming up my frozen body with an energy I'd never felt before. How dare he sound so fucking happy about seeing me in the pitiful condition he'd put me in? I started squirming, trying to free myself from my bonds. I wanted so badly to shout at him. To call for help. I tried to shout out 'Fucking bastard' as loudly as I could, but all that came out was a very muffled effort. The rags in my mouth were tied too tightly.

'Hey,' Jack said, a chuckle in his voice. 'Stop moving around, Ellen. You'll hurt yourself.'

His words just made me all the more determined to free myself, get the fuck out of wherever I was, and go straight to the police. As soon as I'd heard his voice above me, the remnants of whatever misguided love I'd felt for that psychopath – because that's clearly what Jack was, I understood it now – had turned to a strong hatred. It was strange how quickly it happened. I literally felt like a love gauze was being pulled from my eyes. He needed to be locked up. I now had no doubt that he was responsible for the deaths of his family. He was a cruel murderer. How could I have been so fucking naïve? So blinded?

'I have to go now, Ellen,' Jack said. I heard him begin to slide whatever slab was above the hole I was in across again. 'I just popped back to see whether you were still alive. Oh, and you might want to keep your feet still. There's a very long drop below you, and if you fall off that ledge, your arms won't hold you up for long.'

The grey light vanished, and I was in darkness again.

CHAPTER FORTY-ONE

tter cunt, I thought, as the chilling fear returned. That's exactly what Jack was. And to think that I'd trusted him for so long. Thought the best of him, even fantasised about spending the rest of my life with him. What an idiot I was. I'd been so blind. Pathetic, even. But not anymore.

Suddenly, the memory that had been trying to come through about Jack from when we were younger was blazing in full glory in my mind. Of course, how the hell had I forgotten – or blanked out – such an incident? I remembered it all so clearly now. Me, Sabrina, Jack and Adele had all been playing together in the Bryants' big garden one day after school. Their house had been built on the site of a much older one, and there were still old features from the previous property scattered here and there around the grounds like old walls and things, that made it an exciting playground for us. Jack decided that we should play a game a bit like hide-and-seek, but where he actually took one of us and decided where we should hide, and then that the other two should be the seekers, and try to find where he'd hidden that person.

'Come on, Adele,' I remember him saying, his eyes glinting

as he held his hand out towards his little sister. 'I'll hide you first. Sabrina and Ellen, you both go into the kitchen and count to fifty slowly. Then come and try and find Adele. Okay?'

'Okay,' we shouted as we ran back up towards the house.

'You'll never be able to find her,' I remember Jack calling after us.

'Yeah, yeah,' Sabrina shouted back. She was used to her brother bragging about things.

So Sabrina and I did as we'd been instructed to do. We counted to fifty slowly in the kitchen, then went out into the garden and started searching for Adele. Jack was sauntering around the lawn by then, his hands in his pockets, whistling a merry tune.

'No clues,' he said to us. 'I'm not helping you at all. You'll just have to look really closely.'

And we did. Sabrina and I searched in all the usual hiding places first, then scoured every inch of the garden looking for Adele. We even looked in spots that would have been too small for a child to hide in.

'Jack,' Sabrina said after a while, wiping her brow crossly. 'Have you hidden Adele in the house? We've looked everywhere. She's not out here.'

Jack just laughed.

'No, she's not in the house,' he said. 'Adele is definitely somewhere in the garden, I promise you. Now, no more clues. You two are useless at this. You just haven't looked in the right place yet.'

We searched for another half an hour, looking up into the branches of the trees, behind hedges, in the shed, searching places we'd already looked at. But Adele wasn't anywhere.

'Children, time to come back inside. Ellen's mother has just arrived to pick her up,' Penelope called from the back door a little while later.

Despite my protestations about needing to find Adele, Mum bundled me into the car, saying she had chicken cooking in the oven at home and that it would burn if we didn't hurry up and leave. So I wasn't there when the Bryants eventually found Adele.

Sabrina told me about it during school the next day. It turned out that Jack had stuffed his young sister into an old well that was at the back of the garden behind the shed. The ledge she had to balance on was tiny. He'd then pulled the manhole cover back over the entrance to the well, telling his sister that if she dared to scream or draw attention to herself then he'd come back and push her off the ledge, and that she would go plummeting to her death in the deep hole below her. Sabrina was pale-faced and shaking as she described what had happened, how scared and traumatised Adele had been when their mother eventually pulled her out – after threatening to tell Dalton if Jack didn't confess to the whereabouts of his sister.

'We won't tell your father about this,' Penelope had apparently said, as she changed her shaking daughter into dry clothes, while trying to sooth her sobs. 'I don't think there will be any need for that.' Perhaps she feared that her husband would do something even worse to Jack, if he found out what had gone on that afternoon. But the upshot of the situation was that Jack's actions went unpunished and were quickly swept under the rug by the other members of the family.

I remember, now, being very shocked when Sabrina had told me about what Jack had done to Adele. It didn't seem like him, he and his siblings usually got on so well, and even looked out for each other. Why would he suddenly do something like this that had terrified the poor girl so much? Sabrina told me that Jack had said he didn't mean to harm Adele, and that he'd just got carried away with the game. She seemed so fine with it, that I became fine with it too. And I pushed the incident out of my mind, burying any concerns that it may have flagged up. Until now. Clearly burying people below ground level was Jack's MO.

An image of my lovely mum suddenly flashed through my mind. Hot tears sprang out of my eyes and tumbled down my frozen cheeks. How could I have ever wanted the Bryants to adopt me, when I already had a brilliant mum of my own? I'd never properly appreciated her until this point, I realised. I'd been too hard on her, criticised her emotions too much. When all she'd been trying to do was to cope with my dad leaving, and how awful she'd felt afterwards. I'd developed a tainted vision of what a perfect family was; I'd thought that the Bryants personified it. But actually, they were all fucked up. And my family – with all its flaws – was really the perfect one. The one I yearned for now, and needed so badly. I'd even put up with my brother Tom punching my arm for the rest of my life if I made it out of here. There was absolutely no way that I was going to allow Jack to rip my family apart, like he'd already done to his own. He was toxic. No, more than that, he was a sadistic, selfish killer. I had no idea how he'd done it, but the fact that he'd tied me up in a hole meant that he was more than capable of finishing off his own family somehow. Clever, conniving bastard. But there was no way in hell that I was just going to give up the fight and die in some fucking drain, just so Jack could get his hands on the money – the inheritance – that he so obviously and desperately wanted. Because what else would all this be about? I'd always known he was lazy, but it was a characteristic I'd chosen to overlook. He'd probably never written anything of worth in his life. All that bullshit about being a writer, I couldn't believe I'd drunk it all in, believing that he must be some undiscovered literary genius. His aunt, Marjorie, had been right. I should have listened to her more carefully. I should have avoided Jack altogether after I'd spoken to her, and never gone back to my flat. I knew that now. But like the blinded idiot that I was, the magnetic pull that I'd felt towards the man had still been there, and I'd thought it had meant something. Even after hearing everything that Marjorie had to say, I hadn't quite been able to sever the ties that I felt with Jack. I'd gone back to my flat subconsciously hoping that he'd appear with a reasonable explanation, so that I didn't have to believe his aunt. So that I could keep being in love with him, and that in some way, this horrific situation would work itself out. God, I was stupid. But not anymore. The old, blinded Ellen was gone. My eyes were open now.

My hands were going numb with cold and pain. I knew that it was only a matter of time before I lost feeling in them altogether. *Right, Ellen Waldron,* I told myself. *It's time for you to do something amazing. You're going to save yourself. And then go and find the police and tell them all about what Jack's done. And you're not going to stop trying until you're out of this fucking hole. Okay?*

Okay, I agreed with myself. *Let's do this. Pathetic Ellen is a thing of the past. I'm going to be so unbelievably strong from now on.*

Keeping my feet as still as I could on the ledge, I bent my fingers and started trying to feel around. *Wire,* I thought. *That's what he's tied my hands up with. Wire has an end. I just need to find it somehow...*

CHAPTER FORTY-TWO

I don't know how long it took, time lost all it's meaning in that hole. I worked away, gradually feeling around my wrists with the restricted movements that were available to my fingers. I found that if I clenched my hands as much as possible, my fingertips had a bit of agency and could feel the different layers of the wire bound around my wrists. Slowly, gradually, I got to know these layers. Every now and again, I had to stop and breathe deeply. I knew my wrists were now lacerated because of the pain that was getting worse and worse, it was an inevitable part of the process, because the more I moved my hands, the more the wire cut into my flesh. But I was willing to sacrifice a few skin layers for potential freedom. If the pain and the icy cold was getting too much, I'd just make myself remember Jack's cheerful voice as he looked down at me. And I'd force myself to remember the bodies of his family; all grey and dead. And then the hot anger would rise up in me, and I would have renewed strength to carry on.

The thought of getting out of the dripping hell hole was keeping me going. The stink of natural decay was overpowering, and the sensation of claustrophobia was almost too much to bear. I was also thinking about how I would feel when I finally told the police about what Jack had done. When everyone knew the truth about him and what he was really like on the inside. That he wasn't at all the fabulous person I'd thought he was, but in fact was the exact opposite. Evil and cruel.

Okay Ellen, I thought. *This is good, you're doing well. Now all you have to do is find a way to unwrap your wrists. Think of Houdini. It might seem impossible, but nothing is impossible if you really put your mind to it...*

CHAPTER FORTY-THREE

After what seemed like hours of trying to find the end of the fucking wire, I was ready to give up. I was beyond cold, wet, terrified and exhausted. I'd used up the last drop of my energy, and I hadn't achieved what I was so desperate to do. I couldn't go on, I was spent. Done. Jack had achieved what he wanted; he'd broken me. He'd proved that he was stronger than me, that he could just dispose of me like a dirty tissue in a bin. Maybe that's all I was worth.

Maybe I am actually going to die down here, I thought, as I relaxed my poor, cut-up hands and wrists. *Maybe this is it. There's nothing else I can do now. If I can't get myself free from these binds, there's no way I can even begin to try and escape.*

Tears began falling down my cheeks. I didn't want to die. Okay, so maybe I hadn't lived my life to the fullest that I could have done, but I knew that I would now, if I ever managed to escape from this pit, this hellish dungeon.

Please, I pleaded with the universe in my mind. *Just give me one more shot at leading a normal life. I'll grab it with both hands this time. I won't let you down...*

Oh for God's sake, Ellen, I told myself. *Stop being so fucking*

154

pathetic. Stop being such a wimp and expecting everyone else to do things for you. Now you're even hoping that some metaphysical force will step in and help you. Get an actual fucking grip. You've spent your whole life on the outskirts of things, never really putting much effort into anything. Never pushing yourself to find out how much you could succeed. Stop making excuses for doing nothing. For achieving hardly anything. How about you pull the stops out and you help yourself for once? Solve your own problems? Just stop whining and give it another proper go.

So, with anger – mostly at myself – now rushing through me, I steeled my wrists, and once again began looking for the end of the goddamn wire...

I was going to do my utmost to get out, I thought, wishing that I was already out of this damp, dripping gloom. And when I was free, I was going to go straight to the police and tell them exactly what Jack had done to me. That I was in no doubt that he was also responsible for hanging his family members. That they needed to catch him and lock him up forever.

Soon I could feel, if not see, that streams of blood were pouring down my arms from my wrists and fingers. I could even smell it – it had a metallic edge to it – which mingled in with the disgusting mouldy damp smell coming from the wall I was so closely pushed up against. But I didn't care. My body could bleed as much as it wanted, if it meant that I was getting closer to being free. The more I worked away at the wires, the less freezing I felt.

Good work, Ellen, I kept telling myself. *You're doing really well. Just keep going...*

Seconds, minutes, hours went by. Sometimes I wondered if I was in a dream. *Perhaps this could just be a nightmare*, I thought more than once. *I mean, I'd been having those awful*

*hanging dreams often enough since finding the Bryants' bodies –
what if this was another, more graphic, one of those?*

But the pain in my wrists put paid to that theory. If this was
a nightmare, I would have woken myself up by now. A wave of
crying took me over and I had to pause in the midst of my
endeavour. How the fuck had life come to this? Was this really
my punishment for falling in love with a psychopath?

Fucking pull yourself together Ellen, I shouted internally.
*This is no time for victim talk. You've done enough of that in
your life, haven't you? Now's the time to be strong and to find out
what you're really made of. Come on, no slacking. You have to get
this done before Jack comes back. Don't stop, just keep going.*

So that's what I did...

CHAPTER FORTY-FOUR

I managed it. Eventually. After the grey glimmers of light coming through the slab above me had faded to pitch blackness, and after I'd nearly died from pain and the freezing wet conditions several times, I managed to completely prise the rings of wire away from my wrists. Anger turned to elation. As I slipped my hands out of the coils, and brought them down to my mouth, where I breathed as much hot air over them as I could – trying to get some feeling back – I knew that the wetness on them, and the drips going up my sleeves, weren't just from the rain drops getting in through the seams or the dampness of wherever I was. It was my own blood. My wrists were in a bad state now, but they would heal in time. Then I managed to pull the gag out of my mouth, and lower it down until it hung like a thin, tight scarf around my neck. My life was at stake, but I was doing well, I reminded myself. Now, it was a race against time to find a way out of my prison, before Jack came back and found that I'd freed myself. I couldn't afford to stand around feeling sorry for myself, I had to get on with it. I'd already decided that there was no point in calling for help, because if Jack was about

157

and he heard me, it would make him very angry. And I had no doubt that he would kill me if he realised I was putting up any resistance to his sick plan. I'd already patted myself down, and gingerly felt in all my pockets for my phone. But of course, it wasn't there. There was no sign of my bag either. Jack wasn't that stupid, he must have taken them, the bastard.

Turning, very, very slowly, I became aware of the increased danger I was in. Because now that I was no longer tied up by my wrists, there was nothing that would hold me up if my feet slipped off the slimy ledge I was on. One wrong move would result in a very unpleasant death, I was in no doubt about that. I didn't know what was at the bottom of the hole I was suspended over, but if it was water or stone, I wouldn't survive the fall. And no one would know I was there. And Jack would have won.

A massive shot of adrenaline pumped through me. *Fuck Jack*, I thought. *He thinks he has so much power over other people. He thinks he can stick me in this pit and get me out of the way. Well, we'll see about that. If this is a man-made hole or drain, there must be a way in and out for whoever needs to use it.*

I raised up my hands – which now had hot pins and needles in them – and started feeling all over the slimy wall that I was standing right next to. *Yuck*, I thought, as the smell of rotten vegetation got stronger as I dislodged it. It stank, but I didn't care. I didn't care about anything except for getting out of the hole and moving myself to safety. *Come on, Ellen, you have to do this...*

Then I felt it, a metal rung, firmly attached to the wall. I grabbed hold of it. Never had I been so thankful to find something before in my life. I was safer now. If my feet slipped I had something that would keep me safe. *Right,* I thought. *If there's one rung, there must be more.* Holding the one I'd found as tightly as my poor fingers would allow, I carefully lifted up a foot, and brushed it all over the wall until I found what I was looking for. Another rung.

Okay Ellen, you can do this, I told myself. *There will be enough rungs attached to this wall to allow you to climb up it. And you have to do it fast, before Jack comes back...*

CHAPTER FORTY-FIVE

It must have taken a good twenty minutes for me to work my way up that wall. I was singing songs in my head – mainly Ed Sheeran ones – to calm myself down, but my body knew what danger I was in, and I couldn't stop shaking. I was aware that this was a life or death situation, and that Jack could come back at any moment. Or that I could slip and fall. But I kept going, and eventually arrived under the stone slab that I'd heard Jack pulling back and forth.

Summoning all the strength that I had left in me, I raised an aching arm up, and used my hand to push the slab away. It was a slower process than I would have liked, but it worked. I dragged myself through the hole, and up and out.

Shit, Ellen, you've done it! I was so pleased I could have cried, but I knew I had to keep going. So I stamped some feeling back into my poor legs, which were threatening to go totally useless and numb, and made my way blindly from the hole of hell.

I was in some alley, I realised. I had no idea which one, as they all looked the same, even in the daylight. They were all narrow, and were lined by the fences at the end of people's gardens. Some had high trees sticking up over them, and some were lined with bushes. There was only one way in and one way out of all of them, so if Jack decided to come back to check on me, there would be no escape if we ran into each other. And I was feeling very weak now. But I'd come this far, and I was determined to keep going. Rest would come later. Much as I wanted to go to my mum's and fall into her arms, I knew I had to get to safety and call the police.

With a dull shimmer of moonlight radiating down from behind the clouds, I set off into the black night, not knowing where the fuck I was going, or whether Jack was going to find me before I got there...

CHAPTER FORTY-SIX

W as I going the right way? I wondered, staggering a bit as I tried to pump enough feeling back into my legs. I willed them to carry me forwards. *I need you now*, I told them. *Please don't give up on me just yet.*

But how the fuck did I avoid bumping into Jack? I had no idea which direction he would be coming from, if he decided to come back and check on me, gloat over me in the little prison he'd put me in. Sheer terror washed through me as I imagined him finding me, all weak and injured, in the alley. I couldn't face the thought of being stuffed back down that hole again. It had been horrific down there, I'd never felt so helpless in all my life. Oh God, I never wanted to see that man again. The thought that he could do something like that to me was too much to bear.

The fresh air smelled so good after being down in that hole for so long. Its cold edge was delicious, and I breathed it in greedily. The deep breaths helped with my panic, my utter fear that Jack might step out from the shadows and stuff me back down into that pit of despair. Or worse, finish me off for good.

This thought filled my head with dizziness, and for a second I thought I was going to collapse.

Come on Ellen, I said to myself. *You've come this far, you're out of that horrible place now. So just keep going until you find safety. That's it, one foot in front of the other...*

CHAPTER FORTY-SEVEN

Maybe I should try and climb over a hedge, I thought as I walked. I'd tried to run, but it hadn't worked, my legs had folded up beneath me and I'd ended up in a crumpled heap on the stone path. If I could just get into someone's garden, I could knock on their back door and ask for help...

I hadn't found anywhere where this would be possible so far. The fences were all too high. But the good thing was that my eyes had adjusted to the darkness, and I could more or less see where I was going. The alley was quite narrow, as they all were around the town. Maybe four feet wide at the most. Unsurprisingly, it was deserted. Not many people tended to use them after dark, for obvious reasons. Now, if only I could get my bearings... Was I going the right way, or had I been trekking in the wrong direction the whole time?

Then I saw it, the spire of St Peter and St Paul's church that stood looking down over Buckingham. Thank God that some amazing person always kept it illuminated. That spire must have acted like a guiding post for people throughout history. If I walked towards the spire, then I would find civilisation, and people with phones who would help me. So I turned right and walked – as fast as my injuries would allow – towards it.

That's when I heard the footsteps behind me...

CHAPTER FORTY-EIGHT

I didn't know what to do. Fear made me stand still.

Please don't be Jack, please don't be Jack, I kept thinking. I pressed myself into the bush that was next to me, as though it was capable of hiding me from whoever it was.

The footsteps were getting closer.

Then I heard a woof, and turned to see a man walking his dog.

'Excuse me?' I said, lunging towards him. 'Please can you help me?'

The man glanced at me. To be fair, I must have looked like a right state. I had dirt and blood all over me, and probably wasn't the sort of person someone wanted to meet on a dark night. Buckingham had its fair share of crimes, like all towns, and maybe I looked like someone who committed half of them.

'Please?' I said again, my voice louder this time. 'Have you got a phone I can use?'

But the man kept walking until he'd passed me.

"Don't leave me," I shouted, crying now. I felt frantic, I'd never needed help so badly before in my life. "Please. Stop. Come back."

But the man seemed to be speeding up, wanting to get away from me. Obviously my desperation had freaked him out. Soon he was gone, disappearing into the darkness.

Fuck, I thought. *I have to keep going anyway. There'll be more people, once I reach the town...*

And I did keep going, always on high alert, terrified that Jack was going to come round the next bend in the alley.

But then I saw some car lights passing, and knew I was nearing the end.

'Help!' I shouted, walking as quickly as I could.

'Please help me, someone. I've been attacked!'

CHAPTER FORTY-NINE

But the car drove on.

I staggered forward a few paces, looking up and down the pavement, trying to work out where the hell I was. Usually, I knew Buckingham like the back of my hand. But now, I felt disorientated, like I'd just landed on another planet.

It was a couple coming out of a nearby pub – The Star, as I later realised, I'd come out in a completely different part of Buckingham to where my flat was – that found me.

'Are you okay?' the young woman asked, a horrified look on her face.

From then on, things became a bit of a blur. I managed to tell the man and the woman that I'd been attacked, and they called an ambulance and stayed with me till it arrived. Two police officers arrived too, and I told them what Jack had done.

'DS Moretti will meet you at the hospital,' one of them told me, after he'd made a call and reported what I'd told him. Before I knew what was happening, I was in the back of the ambulance being whisked off to Milton Keynes University Hospital.

In the bright artificial light inside the vehicle, I was able to see the extent of the injuries to my wrists. The lacerations were deep, and my arms were stained with blood.

'Just try and relax,' the kind paramedic said as she saw me looking at my red hands. 'You're safe now.'

I gave her my mum's number, and she phoned her for me – as my hands appeared to have stopped working completely.

'She'll meet us at the hospital,' the paramedic said, smiling, as she put her phone back into her pocket. 'Don't worry, you're going to be okay now, Ellen.'

Hearing her kind, comforting tone undid the survival lock I'd had myself in, since climbing out of the hole. The tears started flowing, and once they did, I couldn't stop them. Before I knew what was happening, I was shaking and crying, as though I'd never stop.

'That's right, let it all come out,' the paramedic said, as I convulsed into hysteria. 'You've been through an awful trauma, but it's over now. You're safe now, Ellen.'

Am I though? I was thinking. *Is anyone really safe until the police catch Jack?*

CHAPTER FIFTY

M um arrived soon after I'd been settled into a cubicle in the accident and emergency department.

'Oh love,' was all she could say when she popped her head round and saw me. Seconds later, she'd enveloped me in the biggest bear hug, taking care not to touch my raw wrists and hands.

'You were right,' was all I could sob into her shoulder. 'You were right about Jack, Mum. I should have listened to you.'

'Hey,' she whispered into my hair, 'don't worry about that now, Ellie. The important thing is that you're okay. And you're in the best place now. Everyone here is going to look after you.'

I could hear DS Moretti's voice outside the cubicle. He must have been chatting to the officers who'd followed behind the ambulance in their car.

'Ellen?' he called, a few minutes later. 'Is it okay if I come in and have a quick chat with you?'

I nodded, and Mum called out for him to enter.

Between sobs, I told the detective everything that had happened. How I'd spoken to Marjorie, the fact that Jack had lied about the coroner's verdict, how he'd arrived back at the flat and shown me the papers about Marjorie contesting his dad's will, how I'd decided to take a shortcut to Mum's house, and then how someone – Jack – had hit me over the head. And how I'd woken up tied up in some drain.

'You have great courage, Ellen,' DS Moretti said. 'The way you got yourself out of that situation is nothing less than remarkable. You should be very proud of yourself.'

I looked at Mum and saw that she had tears running down her cheeks. For some reason, seeing her as upset as this made my own sobs subside for a minute.

'I didn't want Jack to win,' was all I could say, my voice coming out thick and muffled-sounding.

'And he won't,' DS Moretti said. 'I have several armed officers out looking for him right now. I just need to ask you a few questions, Ellen...'

I answered everything that the detective asked as best I could. Told him what Jack was wearing – black jeans, a grey hoodie and his suede jacket – and described everything I remembered about the drain Jack had put me in, and the alley around it.

'Is there anyone else that you think Jack might contact now?' DS Moretti said. 'Anyone at all who he's close to? Who might be helping him at the moment, or who could tell us any additional information about where he might be?'

'Layla,' I said. 'Layla Carter. I saw them together before.'

A look of surprise washed across DS Moretti's face.

'Ah, well that helps explain things,' he said. 'Unfortunately Layla Carter was found unconscious in the graveyard in Buckingham, earlier today. She's in the intensive care unit in this hospital – a few floors up from you – right now. She has such bad swelling in her brain, at the moment the doctors are unsure whether she'll ever regain consciousness.'

CHAPTER FIFTY-ONE

A fresh torrent of tears started falling down my cheeks as soon as I heard what the detective had told me. I mean, I've never liked Layla, she's never been very nice to me. But she didn't deserve to get injured to that extent. To be honest, I wouldn't have wished any injury on her at all. The extent of Jack's brutality was truly shocking. I had no doubt that he was behind Layla's attack. He'd shown his true colours and the depths that he was prepared to sink to, in order to try to save himself and his stupid inheritance. But he'd fucked up any chances of that now, hadn't he? Oh God, if only the police could catch him...

A nurse came bustling into the room at that point holding some cream-coloured bandages.

'Right, Ellen,' she said, her face kind but tired. 'Let's get your wrists sorted, shall we? And then the doctor wants you to go for a CT scan, as your head took quite a whack earlier. We just need to make sure it's all okay inside.'

'I'll be in touch very soon.' DS Moretti gave me a quick smile, then nodded at Mum. 'And two officers are going to stay with you in the hospital. Jack Bryant is a dangerous individual who needs to be apprehended with the utmost haste. And we want you to feel as safe as possible, Ellen, hence the police presence here.'

I couldn't talk, so Mum thanked him. The nurse was getting some sort of needle ready beside me.

'You'll just feel a quick jab,' she was saying. 'I'm going to give you some local anaesthetic before I do your stitches. Your right wrist in particular is cut quite deeply, and it will be a much more comfortable procedure for you when the anaesthetic kicks in.'

Oh God, I thought, shutting my eyes. I hated needles. Usually, I'd be trembling by now, but after the day I'd had, the nurse's needle was just a minor worry. I had much bigger, darker things on my mind. Like, where the hell was I going to go when I left the hospital? There was no way I could go back to the flat. And Jack knew where Mum lived; I didn't want either of us going back to her house until he was caught. Where could we go where he wouldn't find me?

CHAPTER FIFTY-TWO

L ying there on my hospital bed gave me a small chance to process the horror of the day. The fact that my beloved Jack was actually a monster was hitting me in the most raw way possible. Everything I'd lived for over the past few years had been a lie. Jack was a lie. He wasn't this foppish, wannabe writer who was magnetic, charming and good-looking. He'd never cared about me, there had never been a possibility that he would one day turn round and find me super attractive. No amount of weight that I lost could have jogged that one along. Because he was actually a bastard. A manipulative, dangerous human being. I couldn't believe he'd had me fooled for that long.

Or actually, I thought, wincing as I moved one of my wrists, maybe I'd been the one who'd been fooling myself. Been wilfully blind, ignoring the red flags that other people – like my mum – had clearly seen. Maybe that's a parent thing, they can sniff out any bad apples who try to fuck up their child's life. But I hadn't listened to her. I'd even got angry and thought she was unfairly maligning Jack. Jesus, I couldn't even trust my own judgement anymore. I couldn't put any weight on who I wanted to trust, as I obviously had no idea who was a safe person to be around and who wasn't.

And now we were in the sticky situation of trying to work out where we could go, someplace where that monster Jack wouldn't find us. It was all so surreal. So awful. We couldn't go to my dad's, as him and Mum didn't get along, and anyway Jack knew where he lived. In fact, we couldn't stay in Buckingham full stop. I didn't want to. I wanted to be someplace where Jack wasn't. But where did that leave us?

CHAPTER FIFTY-THREE

It was Mum who came up with the idea that we go and stay with her friend Jenny in Towcester for a while. There was no way that Jack would know about Jenny, or where she lived, as I was quite sure I'd never mentioned anything about her to him.

A phone call later, it was all arranged. Mum had managed to contact one of her friends – Gayle – in Buckingham, who said she would pop in to feed Nala every day while we were away. Mum had insisted a while back that I give Gayle a spare key to my flat, in case I ever locked myself out and Mum wasn't home to let me in with her spare key.

'Jenny was so sorry to hear what happened to you, love,' Mum was saying, as I was inspecting the bandages that were now wrapped tightly around my wrists. The nurse had done a good job, and I'd kept my eyes shut for the whole thing. 'She said that we can stay as long as we want; she said she has the room, especially since John died. It's just her and the dogs in that big house now.'

It was past 3am when I was finally discharged by an overworked doctor. The CT scan had shown – thank God –

that there was nothing wrong inside my head, which I'd been hugely relieved at.

'We'll give you a lift up to Towcester,' one of the police officers said. Mum had already explained the plan to them. I smiled at him gratefully; I was starting to feel better – safer – at last.

When we'd collected my painkillers from the twenty-four-hour chemist at the hospital, and I'd got changed into some fresh clothes that Mum had brought with her on the advice of the paramedic who'd spoken to her earlier, we finally found ourselves ensconced in the back of the police car and heading up the A5 towards Towcester.

'That's it, love, have a rest,' Mum said, as I laid my head on her shoulder. 'You deserve one after everything you've been through. I'll wake you up when we get there.'

As I closed my eyes, I could feel my insides relaxing. We were safe, we'd got away from Jack, and there was no way he could find us at Jenny's house. The police were out looking for him, and I was really hoping that by the time I woke up in Jenny's spare room tomorrow, I'd be greeted with the news that he had been caught and was firmly behind bars.

CHAPTER FIFTY-FOUR

Jenny was like our guardian angel – at least that's what she looked like to me – as she opened her front door. We were still in the police car, we hadn't even rung the bell. But she must have seen the car headlights through her window. She must have been waiting, watching out for us to arrive, bless her.

'Darlings,' she said, in her usual theatrical way. 'You poor things. Come in this instant and have a cup of tea. Or something much stronger...'

A few minutes later, we were all sitting round Jenny's little wooden kitchen table. I'd never been to her house before – although Mum had – and I loved it as soon as I stepped through the door. Jenny was someone with exquisite taste, and everything in her house just blended together in a way that made each room a visual delight to behold. The bohemian wall hangings, the shabby chic cupboards, it all went together so well somehow.

I'd spotted a newspaper lying in the porch as I made my way into Jenny's house, and the headline had made me bend down to read the front page. *Girl Found Unconscious in Buckingham Graveyard*, the Towcester Chronicle reported. *A dog-walker made the gruesome discovery of a badly beaten girl as he took his usual jaunt through Buckingham Town...*

'Come on, love,' Mum had said, seeing me staring down at these awful words. 'You don't need to be reading that now. Layla's in the best place that she can be right now, and we just have to hope that she recovers.' She shepherded me past the paper and into the warm house.

'There you go,' Jenny said, placing a thick sandwich in front of me as I slumped over the table. 'Get your chops round that. You must be starving. You've been through such a horrific nightmare today.'

When I met her gaze, I saw that her eyes were worried. But she was smiling, so I attempted a grin back. I picked up the sandwich and took a little nibble. But my stomach was still in knots, the fear that I'd felt as I'd awoken and found myself prisoner down that drain had caused an overwhelmingly acidic feeling in my gut.

I shut my eyes once more, as I listened to Mum and Jenny's soothing voices. They weren't discussing what had happened to me that day, although I knew Mum probably wanted to. They were making light chit-chat. Probably so as not to upset me, and I was very grateful for that.

'Ellie,' Mum put her hand on my knee, 'Why don't you go up to bed, love. You look shattered. You could do with a really good rest.'

'Ah, good idea.' Jenny stood up from the table as I opened my eyes. 'Come with me, darling. I've given you the most comfy bed in the house. Memory foam mattress; you'll sleep like a baby.'

As I dragged my aching body into a standing position, I had no idea how I was going to make it up the stairs. But I had to, had to reach that pillow, as my eyes were shutting again, and my body needed sleep so badly...

CHAPTER FIFTY-FIVE

I opened my eyes to the most thumping headache I'd ever experienced in my life. Jesus, I needed some painkillers, but I couldn't move. My whole body ached, and my wrists felt like they'd been sliced with glass fragments.

'Oh hello, Ellie.' Mum had popped her head round the door. 'I've been checking on you all day. You've had a good sleep.'

'All day?' I said, feeling groggier than I ever had before. What I was experiencing was much worse than a hangover. A hangover times ten thousand. I felt beyond exhausted already, and I'd only just woken up.

'Yes, it's about quarter past three in the afternoon,' Mum said, going over to open the curtains. 'And it's actually sunny for once.'

As I watched the sun's rays spill into the room, I suddenly felt a huge appreciation for life in a way that I never had before. It was like I was properly seeing the sun for the first time, and understanding how amazing it was. How wonderful literally everything in my life was. Except for Jack...

'Have they caught him?' I said.

'No, love.' Mum's brow wrinkled. 'DS Moretti called about

an hour ago. He said that he has his best officers searching for him, and that they're not going to give up the hunt until they've found and arrested him. Don't worry, Ellie, you're safe here at Jenny's. There's no way Jack would know to look here. You can relax now, love. I'm sure we'll hear some good news soon.'

I was quiet for a minute, thinking. Yes, Mum was probably right. There was no way Jack would know that I was here. But all of a sudden flashbacks of being in that hole flitted through my brain and body, and for a moment it felt like I was back down there. Icy fear took a hold of me, and I shut my eyes tight, wincing.

'Oh Ellen, are you okay?' I could hear Mum walking towards me. 'Do you want some of those painkillers?'

I nodded, and heard her footsteps leave the room.

Jack might not be my problem anymore, but the injuries and memories that he'd left me with were clearly going to be around for a while.

That's Jack, I thought, turning over. *Some fucking best friend you turned out to be, you bastard.*

CHAPTER FIFTY-SIX

I spent the hour of daylight that was left just gazing out of Jenny's back window, enjoying the soothing sight of the rolling Northamptonshire fields. Every now and again, a train would chug by in the distance, and I would wonder what people were on it, and where they were going. It seemed strange that the rest of the world was just going about its daily business, as though nothing had happened. But it was also a comforting notion. Other people's lives went on as normal, even when yours was collapsing around you.

But it's not collapsing anymore, I thought, briefly looking down at my bandaged wrists. *Jack didn't win, I did. He thought he could control me, but I didn't let him. I'm stronger than I ever knew...*

As I watched the sky turn dark grey, I couldn't help thinking how happy I was to be alive. Coming so close to death and then surviving the situation had given me a sort of euphoric rush, that was interrupted by intermittent bouts of fear that Jack would somehow find me. But how could he?

I stayed at the windowsill until the fields had become just a black space at the back of the house. Then I stood up very slowly – my body ached as though it had been hit by a fast train – and turned my head towards the delicious smells coming out of the kitchen.

Ah, I thought. *A bit of normality. Some home cooking. Now that's definitely what the doctor ordered...*

CHAPTER FIFTY-SEVEN

By five o'clock that evening, when the autumnal darkness had taken over the sky once again, I was feeling a lot better. The strong painkillers, which turned out to be co-codamol – a mixture of codeine and paracetamol – were kicking in, and I'd downed two bowls of Jenny's home-made chicken broth, which had helped to warm my insides. She was a damn good cook. We'd eaten a sandwich when we'd got to Jenny's the previous evening – although I couldn't manage much of mine. I just couldn't stomach it after the horrendous ordeal I'd gone through. But when I'd eventually got out of bed at around four that day, in one of Jenny's prettily decorated spare bedrooms, my stomach had growled loudly and reminded me that it actually needed some proper food in it.

Because I'd never actually been to Jenny's house before I wasn't aware that she didn't actually live in the town of Towcester, it turned out that she actually lived in a small village about three miles outside it called Grafton Regis. Jenny had told me how she and her husband John had bought a plot of land there many years ago and built a beautiful stone cottage at the end of a long gravel drive, a little further down the hill from most of the houses in the village. It was a lovely spot, just the right sort of place to stay at and convalesce, I decided. Remote enough to feel like you'd got away from the hustle and bustle of town life, but a close enough drive to shops and amenities to ensure that you could easily buy anything you needed.

'How are you feeling, Ellen?' Jenny sat down in the chair opposite me. We were in her cosy kitchen, and she'd just drawn the curtains and placed beautiful-smelling candles along the windowsill. Jenny had been a colleague of Mum's many years ago, when they'd both worked in a primary school – Jenny as a teacher and Mum as her assistant. They'd got on really well and stayed in touch ever since, and I remember Mum being very sad when John – Jenny's husband – had died from a heart attack about three years before. Jenny was a bit older than Mum, and had quite a bohemian air about her. She always wore beaded necklaces and earrings, and had quite an eye for beautiful scarves that she wore wrapped round her bobbed hair. I'd always liked her; she had a timeless feel about her, very wise, like she was an old soul who'd visited the Earth many times before.

'Better than when I woke up,' I said, managing a small grin. 'Thanks so much for having me and Mum to stay at such short notice. It's really kind of you.'

'Oh, no trouble at all,' Jenny said. 'It's nice to have some company for once. Usually it's just me and those naughty dogs these days.'

As if on cue, one of her Bichon Frises, Bertie, came waddling into the kitchen, and sat himself down on my foot.

'Probably hoping you'll drop some crumbs for him to hoover up,' Jenny said. 'Sorry, old boy, you're out of luck. Ellen's finished her food. And anyway, you're quite fat enough. You don't need feeding up any more.'

'Where's Mum?' I said, half annoyed with myself that I'd

regressed back to some sort of co-dependent state since Jack's attack on me yesterday. I felt like I just needed to know where she was at all times at the moment, to help me stay feeling safe.

'Oh, she's just popped outside to get a magazine out of my car,' Jenny said, smiling. 'While you were eating your broth in here, we were in the living room chatting about how all three of us could maybe go on a holiday together next summer – I think we'll all deserve one quite honestly, especially you – and I said I had a magazine in the car with some great reviews of Barbados in it. Your mum offered to go and get it. She must have found something about my car quite interesting, as she's been a little while now.'

A spike of fear jolted through me. Why had she been a little while? *Now Ellen*, I told myself, *Mum is probably absolutely fine. Jack doesn't know that either of you are here. Yes, but I'll just go and check on her anyway*, I replied to myself. *Just to make sure she's okay.*

I stood up slowly, and told Jenny that I was going outside to say hi to Mum, and to get some fresh air.

'Okay darling,' she said. 'Good idea. Nothing like a bit of cold air to clear the head.'

With my heart racing faster, I walked to the front door and pushed it open. Mum must have left it on the latch so that she could get back in after she'd picked up the magazine.

'Mum?' I called, stepping out onto the gravel drive and immediately feeling the impact of the cold night air through my pyjamas. 'Mum? Where are you?'

CHAPTER FIFTY-EIGHT

There was no answer. Which was very strange, as Mum knew how wobbly I was feeling at the moment, both emotionally and physically. Usually she would have replied straight away, to put my mind at rest.

Jenny's car was parked round the side of the house, so with my slippers making loud crunching sounds on the gravel, I made my way round there in the freezing night air, sure that I'd find her reading the magazine in the car or something. She could be a bit absent-minded sometimes, so it's something she might well have ended up doing. She'd probably got absorbed in reading an article...

'Mum?' I called again, rounding the corner of the house.

Then I saw him. Jack. Holding a knife up to my mum's neck. Some sort of sports bag slung over his shoulder. I stood still, immediately filled with dread and fear. *How the absolute fuck did he find us at Jenny's house?*

'Let her go, Jack,' I said. I hesitated for a moment, then walked towards him. Arctic chills of terror were screaming through me as I looked from my mum's terrified face to Jack's insane one. 'It's me you want, not my mum. Just let her go, and then you and me can talk.'

'You forgot that I had your phone, didn't you?' Jack said, a grim smile on his face. He had a black rucksack slung over one of his shoulders, I noticed. 'Silly girl. You should have remembered that I could track where your mum's phone was through yours. And obviously I knew that you'd be with her. Well done for escaping from the drain yesterday, by the way. It must have taken some strength and skill to get out of there by yourself. I was impressed, Ellen, when I went back and found it empty.'

He pushed the knife even closer to my mum's throat, and she let out a whimper. I'd always known that I loved my mum, of course. But until that moment, I didn't realise how much, what an all-encompassing energy of devotion, love and protection I felt for her. And there was no way in hell I was going to let Jack hurt her while I had an ounce of breath left in my body.

'Hey Jack,' I said, trying to sound as relaxed as possible, while in reality I was submerged in brain-chilling fear. 'Let go of her, and come and talk to me. She's nothing to you, but I know it's me you want, isn't it? Me who knows too much about what you did to your family?'

Jack twisted his mouth sideways, coming across as droll as ever.

'Yep,' he said. 'You're right.'

He reached down and snatched Jenny's car keys out of my mum's hand, then let go of her neck and pushed her away from him.

'Get in the car, Ellen,' he said in his normal, chatty voice.

'No,' my mum said, trying to come over to me. 'Please Jack. Don't take her again. She's been through too much already.'

Jack was too quick for her. He got to me first. He grabbed

the hair at the back of my head, making me shout out in pain as it was the exact spot where he'd hit me the day before.

'Sorry, old thing,' he said to my mum. 'But your daughter has pissed me right off. And she needs to come with me now. Ta-ta.'

And with that, he opened the front passenger door, shoved me inside, then quickly ran round to get in the driver's side, slinging his bag on to the back seat.

Mum lunged forward and opened the door. But Jack was ready for this. He put his knife to my cheek and slowly sliced it open. It was a surface wound, but it fucking stung. Mum's face crumpled as she watched the blood oozing down my cheek.

'Close the door right now,' he said. 'Or something much worse will happen to your daughter.'

'It's okay, Mum,' I said, even though I knew it wasn't. 'Just do as he says, and I'll be fine. I'll find a way to be fine, like before.'

Mum had no choice. She let out a howl, and shut the door. Jack was already revving up the engine. As he spun the car round and headed for the end of the drive, I turned round to see Jenny running out of the front door, obviously wondering what all the noise was about.

'Now, isn't this nice?' Jack slapped his hand on to my knee as he swung the car out of the drive and on to the country lane. 'It's just you and me now, Ellen. Just as you've always wanted. Oh yes, I've known how you've felt about me for a while. I've read all your diaries, you see. I'm so glad I found you because, boy, have I got a surprise in store for you...'

CHAPTER FIFTY-NINE

I suddenly knew what I was going to do. The thought had come to me in a flash. I was going to throw myself out of the car when Jack slowed down a bit. *Yes,* I thought. *Good thinking, Ellen.* We still weren't very far from Jenny's house, so with a bit of luck Jack would be so surprised at my departure that it would give me enough time to run back. Then we could lock the doors and wait for the police...

We were coming to a junction. With the car now slowing, I took a deep breath, opened my door, and threw myself out. Pain whooshed through me as my body hit the road, I could feel sharp stones and gravel embedding themselves in my skin, and I rolled sideways into a hedge. But I didn't care about any injuries, I just wanted to be as far away from Jack as I possibly could be. Wounds would heal later. So as I heard him shouting, the car screeching to a halt, and his door opening, I got up and started running.

Come on, Ellen, I thought. *Sprint faster than you ever have in your life.*

I tried, I really did. But the gradient was quite steep.

Nevertheless I willed myself on, thinking of Jenny's house, and Mum's open arms...

Pounding footsteps behind me. An angry growl from Jack. His hands grabbing me, turning me round.

'What the fuck do you think you're doing, Ellen?' he said, hissing into my face as he shook me back and forth. 'Did I say you could get out of the car? No I did not. God wants you to be with me right now, Ellen, and you don't have the right to defy his wishes, do you?'

He marched me back to the car, holding my arms so tightly that my skin was burning under his grip.

'Get in,' he said, pushing me roughly into the car before slamming the door. He ran round to his side, got in, and pulled his own door shut.

'My bad,' he said, turning to me. 'I should have put the central locking on shouldn't I?' And he reached out and clicked it into place. The button for this was on his car door, there was no way I could reach it easily.

'Well now,' Jack said, reaching down and retrieving his knife from the footwell, where it must have fallen when he exited the car in such a hurry, 'Let's try again, shall we? And this time, no nasty surprises, thank you, Ellen.' He waved the knife in front of my nose. 'Unless you have a fetish for me using this on you.'

I was shaking uncontrollably as he started up the car, and it wasn't just because of the freezing air. I'd tried to escape and he'd stopped me. And now I couldn't even open the fucking car door. And I didn't have a phone because Jack had taken it the first time he'd kidnapped me. I couldn't contact anyone, I was completely on my own. What the hell was I going to do?

CHAPTER SIXTY

'Where are you taking me?' The adrenaline was back, pumping round my body at full force. I didn't feel in pain in any way, I was in survival mode again. I wiped away the blood that was running down my cheek. I knew that Mum and Jenny would immediately phone the police, tell them what Jack had done, and give them the number plate of Jenny's car which Jack had stolen. There would be people out looking for us within minutes. If I could just keep him talking until they found us...

'You'll find out,' Jack said. I watched a cruel smile spread across his face.

I sat very still for a few minutes, as we bombed too fast down the country roads in the blackness of the night, Jack not seeming to care which way he was turning when we got to junctions. I was wondering how he was going to surprise me – with something no doubt horrendous – if he had no idea where he was going.

'So, why did you come and get me?' I said, trying to keep my tone conversational. 'I mean, I'm not being funny, Jack, but the police already know what you did to me yesterday. And they've found Layla – she's fighting for her life in the intensive care unit. You're already a wanted man. So why do you need me?'

Jack leant his head back and laughed.

'Are you really that stupid, Ellen?' he said. He snapped his head back and looked round at me. It was dark in the car, but I could just about see the glint of malice in his eyes. 'This is all your fault.'

Now it was my turn to want to laugh. Despite the acute danger I knew I was in, I couldn't help feeling disbelief at his ludicrous statement.

'Er, how and why can any of this be my fault?' I said.

'Because you've gone and ruined everything, haven't you, old bean?' Jack said. 'Why couldn't you just keep your nose out of my business? I know it's probably because you love me so much, but really. If you truly loved me, you would have just taken my word for everything and not gone snooping around.'

'Well I don't love you anymore,' I said, the words coming tumbling out before I could stop them. I didn't want to aggravate Jack unnecessarily, but the feelings of hatred and betrayal that I had for him were too strong to be contained. 'So don't worry about that.'

'Ah,' Jack said. 'There's such a thin line between love and hate, as they say. You're so gullible, Ellen. You believe everything that people tell you. You were supposed to be my handy alibi. I've spent weeks working on you, dropping hints here and there that I might reciprocate your feelings, but keeping them vague enough to keep you guessing. That's one of the reasons I moved in with you. I knew you'd be too much of a loner to go out anywhere on your birthday, so as I suspected, we spent the night of your eighteenth watching boring films. As you thought I'd been with you the whole time, you told the police that in no uncertain terms. It was all going perfectly at that stage.'

'What do you mean – *thought* I'd been with you?' I said. 'You were with me that night, Jack.'

'Ha, well, yes I was to start with,' Jack said. 'But didn't you wonder why you fell into such a deep sleep on the sofa? A few of my mother's sleeping pills crushed up in your drink sorted that one out. You were out for the count; it gave me enough time to go back to my family home and do what needed to be done. You were still snoring when I got back. So I just got into bed and fell asleep. I knew you'd be none the wiser when you woke up and found me there, so at that point it was happy days.'

'Wow,' I said, wondering – for the thousandth time over the last twenty-four hours – how I could have ever even liked the man sitting next to me. Yes, Jack was right. There was a thin line between love and hate. But what I now felt for him was a loathing so deep that I would happily kill him, if given half a chance.

'I've been reading your diaries for ages. Almost every time you go out, in fact,' Jack said, with a nonchalance in his voice. 'You're not very good at hiding them, Ellen. No one hides things under their bed if they really don't want anyone to find them. They're quite boring really, you just drone on and on about me most of the time. Which is very flattering, I must say. But obviously, there's no way in hell that I would ever like you in that way.'

'Even though we slept together?' I said.

'Ah, but we didn't,' Jack said with a laugh. 'That was another little ruse, to glue you to me even more. Because I knew that the more besotted you were with me, you would overlook the small details that I couldn't cover up – like Marjorie potentially whining about me to you. I know Sabrina had been running off to see her every now and again, and complaining to her that I was getting too dominant and that she would probably find a way to pass this information on to you at some point. I knew that the more in love with me you became, the more you'd find reasons not to believe my aunt, or anyone else, if they told you bad things about me. I had to keep you sweet, you see, as you were my all-important alibi. I know you better than you know yourself, Ellen. That night when you were passed out drunk, I just took all our clothes off then wanked into a condom and left it on the floor. I have to admit that I do quite like fucking with your head. It's actually quite fun.'

'Hmm,' I said. 'Shame you ruined all your good work by lying about the coroner's verdict. That was what led me to Marjorie in the first place.' An anger was now seething through me. Hearing him so glibly tell me about his psychotic behaviour as though he was the cleverest person in the world was too much.

Jack sucked air in through his teeth.

'Yep, I'll give you that one,' he said. 'I don't think I was thinking straight at that point; I was probably still drunk. I only said that because for a minute I thought I could just make you believe that, and you'd leave the whole thing alone. All I wanted was to inherit the house and the money, and then to move back home and live a quiet life by myself, uninterrupted by any of the idiots in the world. Unfortunately, I turned into one of those idiots myself, the moment I told you that the verdict was suicide. I mean, you're not the brightest button in the box Ellen, but even you were suspicious about that. And you never realised that I'd put that sheet of notepaper from one of my father's pads in my pocket, hoping that you would go snooping around and find it. I knew you wouldn't be able to help yourself, so I pretended to be asleep after I'd woken up – when we'd got really drunk together – hoping that you'd have a good look round. The more sorry you felt for me the better. And you did. Everything was ticking along so nicely, until you went and ruined it.'

We drove through a village, its high street lit up by glowing street lamps. Hardly anyone was about; not that I could have got their attention even if I'd wanted to. Jack had positioned his knife under his knee that was furthest away from me, and I knew he could grab it at any moment. I looked out of the window, and saw that a sign said 'Welcome to Hanslope'. Another pointed the way to a place called Salcey Forest.

'Ah, perfect,' Jack said, also spotting the signs. 'I know exactly where we are going now. Hold tight, Ellen; it won't be long before you'll be getting your surprise...'

CHAPTER SIXTY-ONE

We carried on speeding down empty country lanes, the hedges whizzing by in the light of the car's headlamps. I felt like I was on some nightmare rollercoaster; terror had overtaken any anger that I felt for Jack, and my senses were on such high alert that I was noticing every little detail about the car, the irritating little laughs Jack kept doing, the road in front of us. Oh God, I so badly wanted to wake up and find that this had just been the worst nightmare of my life.

I couldn't believe I'd gone through the whole awful escape from the drain the day before, just to end up with psycho Jack kidnapping me again twenty-four hours later. This kind of thing only happened in the films that my brother Tom liked watching. The relief I'd felt in the back of the ambulance made my current situation all the more insultingly awful. How dare this man try to take such control over my life?

I was starting to think that Jack got off on my fear, so I decided to try to keep my terror inside and not let it show too much. Anything I could do to take his pleasure away, I was going to do it.

I had to keep him talking, I knew I did. Because the longer

he was distracted, the more chance the police had of tracking the car. Obviously there were none of those clever cameras on these country roads that took pictures of number plates and sent them back to some control room. I'd watched a police documentary with Tom about that once. But I had to believe they would find me somehow. I kept checking the wing mirror, hoping to see blue flashing lights behind us. But so far, all I could see was blackness...

CHAPTER SIXTY-TWO

'So that's why you did all of this, why you killed your whole family, because you wanted their house and money?' I said. I knew Jack must be planning something very unpleasant for me, so what did I have to lose by asking him this? My mind was in overdrive, I was trying to work out possible ways to escape from him, to raise an alarm. But I knew that if I just jumped out of the car here he would follow me with his knife... And anyway, he'd already locked all the doors.

'Yep, pretty much,' Jack said. 'And it would have actually worked, if you hadn't decided to turn into Miss Fucking Marple and go snooping around, putting two and two together, Ellen. You're such a liar. You don't love me at all. If you did, you would have protected me, and listened and believed everything I had to say. But instead, you went to see my aunt, and got suspicious. I heard you on the phone to her in the flat, after I showed you the papers about her contesting the will. Stupid bitch wanted to hide the money from me, but there was no way that was going to happen. That's why my family had to go, before she got her way. But I heard you speaking to her, and I could tell from your tone of voice that you were starting to doubt me. I figured that she must have told you why she was contesting the will. If you changed your story to the police about me being home that night – if you told them that you'd actually been asleep for ages – then they might start suspecting me more. You were becoming a hindrance, a liability, which is why I had to get you out of the way.'

'And Layla?' I said. 'What did she do to deserve your attack on her?'

'Ah,' Jack said, with a grin. 'Well that was my fault really. After I'd shagged her in the graveyard, we drank so much that I got a bit loose lipped; told her a bit too much if you know what I mean. I told her how I'd used you, and what fun I'd had drugging your drink on your birthday. When you'd found us, and then disappeared off again in a huff, Layla suddenly put two and two together and realised that I must have done it so that I could go and make sure my family made it to the grave. She knew it was your birthday the day before my family was found, she must have seen your crap little photos of us sitting under duvets watching films on social media that day with your hashtag of *best birthday ever*. I was so drunk and pissed off when Layla started staring at me with wide eyes and screaming that something inside me just snapped. Once I'd started hitting her, I couldn't stop. I had to make her shut up. She was being so loud. It was so annoying.'

I was now only half listening to what the psycho next to me was saying. What had got my attention was the fact that we'd just driven past a sign saying 'You Are Now Entering Salcey Forest'. The car's headlights were now illuminating thick rows of giant fir trees down both sides of the road. It all felt very deserted, and there wasn't another car in sight.

Then Jack pulled the wheel down hard and we drove off the road, through some trees, and into the forest itself. He dimmed the car's headlights, and a shrill fear rose up in me. Because I now knew that he was planning to kill me, and had been looking for a suitably deserted place to do it in. Somewhere that he wouldn't get interrupted. And no doubt his surprise would be my manner of death. Given how sadistic I now knew that Jack was, I fully believed that my death was going to be extremely painful...

CHAPTER SIXTY-THREE

T his was very bad news. The worst kind. Because now that we were driving through these fucking trees, the police wouldn't be able to see the car even if they drove down the road we'd been on.

Keep him talking, Ellen, I told myself. *Okay, so you're now in a fucking forest, but the longer you keep him busy, the more time you buy yourself. And even if it comes to the worst possible outcome, and he tries to attack you, just remember how strong you were yesterday. You kept yourself safe, climbed out of that drain, and found help. There's no reason why you can't do something similar today. Jack's not the genius mastermind he seems to think he is. He's so arrogant, you'll find some way to get out of this.*

My technicolour feeling of sensory overload now doubled. Every single detail on each tree that the car's dimmed lights hit on was not lost on me. My head was tingling with energy. *I could do this, I could do this...*

CHAPTER SIXTY-FOUR

'Something I've been wondering,' I said, as we plunged further into the trees, 'is how on earth you managed to kill all six members of your family like that. I mean, if it wasn't so brutal and evil, I would be impressed.'

'Yes, I thought you might ask me that,' Jack said, driving the car over a bumpy overgrown patch. 'That was down to the power of God, Ellen. Well, God and my dear late father.'

'What do you mean?' Fuck, Jack was clearly even madder than I'd thought. Completely off his rocker.

'I mean,' Jack said, an element of glee coming into his voice, 'that the whole family was already so well-trained to follow instructions in the notebooks by the time that my dad died. When he – Dalton – started speaking through me to them, telling me to continue to write down instructions and what to say, they had no trouble believing it. Well, everybody except Sabrina, that is. She needed a little help to get that noose around her neck, if you know what I mean. She wasn't playing ball, so I had to slap her around a bit, until she submitted and got on with the job in hand. And the fact that in the end I had them all at knifepoint helped rather a lot.'

'Right,' I said, as the car tumbled further into the forest. Was this place never-ending? Jack's words about his sister had made me feel sick. He was so cruel, it defied understanding. 'So you're telling me that you really believe your deceased father was guiding you, Jack? Tell me, do you really, honestly believe that he was doing that? Or were you just manipulating your poor family and lying to them, telling them to do horrible things to themselves, so that you could get the house and the inheritance? Knowing perfectly well that it wasn't your dad speaking through you, that it was just your own selfish brain influencing everyone for your own ends?'

'Woah.' Jack took one hand off the steering wheel and held it out, palm side straight up. 'Steady on, Ellen. Are you really questioning the power of God here? And the ability of our dead loved ones to communicate with us from the other side? Do you really think that we don't go on after we die? I have to disappoint you, if that's actually your belief. I know a lot more about religion, about the Christian faith, than you do, don't I? So it makes sense that I have authority over this. I mean, are you seriously doubting my words?'

'Yes Jack,' I said. I mean, I honestly felt like I had nothing to lose at that point. 'That's exactly what I'm doing. I don't believe a word of this bullshit you keep spinning about hearing your dead father's voice. Either you're psychotic, or you're evil, and I have a strong feeling the truth lies further towards the second concept. All I want you to do is say something honest. Just admit one of the horrific things that you have done to me, without covering it up with this religious crap. Because I want you to prove to me just what a fucking evil, scheming, dishonest bastard you really are.'

'Sorry, old thing,' Jack said, slowing the car down. 'No can do. I'm standing by my story. Whether or not you believe me is really your own problem. If you want to fool yourself about

God, far be it from me to stop you. Not that I actually care, and not that it matters a jot now. Because we've arrived. Perfect spot. Jump out of the car now, Ellen.' He unlocked the car and I jumped at the sudden noise.

'Why?' I said, playing for time. I knew exactly why, but every fibre in my body was screaming that it didn't want to die. I hadn't wanted to yesterday, when he'd stuffed me in the drain, and I didn't now that he'd taken me to this godforsaken forest. Since surviving yesterday's experience, I understood why life was so precious now. I could see how I hadn't been living mine to the fullest. But I got it now, it all made sense. I just wanted the chance to live properly, to take life by the horns and do something wonderful with it. As far as I was concerned, this didn't have to do with going to church and following someone else's rules, it had to do with me realising my potential. And I had now. I didn't want the pathetic excuse for a human being – who went by the name Jack – to ruin my existence any more.

'Because my father has given me another message,' Jack said. 'He's telling me that you're being called home, back to the other side. He said you have to co-operate fully with me, and help to end your own life. He called my own family members home in the same way. My mother practically jumped up on her stool, she was more than ready to go. Granny wasn't far behind her. Me holding the younger ones at knifepoint was enough incentive for them. But Sabrina was the biggest problem. My father had been right, she was getting too independently minded for her own good. She would have caused the biggest barrier between me and my inheritance. But the good thing is that she's where she should be now. And if it wasn't for you, I'd be receiving the money that is rightfully mine very soon. That's how it goes in proper families, Ellen. Everything goes to the firstborn son, i.e. me. Unfortunately my father chose not to see it that way, which is why he had to go first. He needed to be out of the way before I could deal with everyone else. Now, it's your duty to be co-operative, Ellen. Don't let the Lord down. Don't be like my sister, Sabrina. She was very badly behaved at the end. I'd advise you to learn from her mistakes. Be a good girl. So go on, out you get...'

CHAPTER SIXTY-FIVE

I sat very still for a moment, thinking. Of course I was right, Jack was planning to kill me. Although I hadn't expected him to say that I should be complicit in my own death. If I was in such danger, I had everything to gain from attempting to escape from this monster. I had to believe it would work, that I could do this, that my one last chance at preserving my own life might mean something. I'd done it before, hadn't I? I'd managed to climb out of that fucking awful drain that Jack had put me in? *You can do this Ellen*, I told myself. *Just focus.* Also, he'd admitted to me how he'd managed to finish his whole family off in one go. This was vital evidence, and I had to get to DS Moretti to tell him. Jack was a danger to society. He needed to be stopped...

My eyes went to the door handle. Jack had undone the central locking system; he wanted me to get out so he could arrange my death. But if I opened it fast enough...

In one swift movement, I opened the car door, threw myself out, and ran blindly into the darkness.

Footsteps immediately pounded behind me.

'Stupid bitch,' Jack hissed into my ear, as he grabbed a

clump of my hair. 'Stop trying to get away from me. Didn't you learn anything from the first time that you tried this little trick? Silly girl. Stop acting out and just behave, will you?'

I turned, and in the dim light of the moon that was filtering through the trees, I made out his shape. *Yes, Jack, I have learned something from the first time I tried this,* I thought. I lifted my leg up and kicked him as hard as I could in the balls.

As he groaned and crumpled, I tore my hair away from his grasp – feeling it rip from my head. Pain was nothing to me anymore.

Then I turned, and ran...

CHAPTER SIXTY-SIX

I hadn't gone far when a searing pain down my left arm forced me to grind to a halt for a moment. In the blackness, I hadn't seen the fucking bramble that had ripped off my bandage and dug its thorns into the injury I'd sustained on my wrist the day before because of the wire Jack had wrapped round me. Thorns surrounded my arm and for the moment it was impossible to move.

Looking over my shoulder, desperately hoping that Jack wouldn't find me while I was delayed, I listened out for footsteps, for any sound that he was approaching.

Oh my God, I thought as I tried to free myself, dizziness overtaking me for a moment. *Don't pass out, don't pass out, I told myself. If you're unconscious you will be a sitting duck and Jack will find you easily. Suck it up and keep going.*

I so badly wanted to scream and shout, the pain I was now in was agonising. *No*, I thought. *Think of getting to safety, Ellen. Think of telling the police about Jack. He might even go back and attack Mum. You have to protect her, you have to keep going.*

Ignoring the fresh blood that was now soaking my arm, I

stepped away from the bramble as quietly and quickly as I could, and set off again...

CHAPTER SIXTY-SEVEN

Just keep going Ellen, I told myself. *Just run as fast as you can.*

So that's exactly what I did, keeping an ear out for pounding footsteps behind me. It was a treacherous business, sprinting through a forest that I'd never been to in my life before in near pitch blackness. The very dim moonlight illuminated some of the trees, but the briary forest floor – crowded with brambles and undergrowth – was a mystery to me. I couldn't make out anything that was underfoot, the only time I could tell was when I'd fallen on top of it.

My legs were getting ripped to shreds from the brambles, sharp twigs and thorns I kept careering into, and every now and again I would trip and fall over some unseen obstacle. My thin pyjamas were no match for the overgrown undergrowth. But I made myself get up and go on and on, the thought of somehow getting to a place of safety inspiring my energy to keep going. The thought of falling into Mum's arms, and of telling DS Moretti what Jack had told me about what he did to his family, spurring me on. Utter bastard. He needed to be taken off the streets, no one was safe with him about.

On and on I went, panting, trying to keep the noise down so that Jack wouldn't find me. *I'm doing well,* I thought. *This is good, Ellen. Keep it up.*

But then – suddenly – I slipped and fell into a deep hole, and the pain in my ankle was so bad it cut through the high levels of adrenaline that were running through me.

'Shit,' I said, under my breath. 'Fuck. It doesn't matter about the pain, Ellen, you need to keep going. Get up now and get on with it. You'll have time to cry later.'

I heaved myself into a sitting position. I was now half covered in mud and other forest debris, and the slipperiness of the sludge was making my progress even slower than it would have been, as I turned and began heaving myself out of the hole. I couldn't put any pressure on my right foot, I found, because that ankle was properly hurting, and I fell every time I tried to make it take my weight.

Then I heard it, a crack of a twig not far from me.

'Oh Ellen,' Jack's voice called. 'Come out, come out, wherever you are...'

CHAPTER SIXTY-EIGHT

I made myself stand up and keep going. It was fall and die, or run and live, as far as I was concerned. The adrenaline pumping through me wasn't enough to keep the stabbing pains in my ankle at bay, but I totally ignored them and ran blindly this way and that, determined to make it out of the forest and on to a road, any road, that would take me to safety.

There were so many hidden obstacles, so many boughs of trees, muddy patches and thorny briars to get past. Because it was so freezing, the branches of the trees seemed extra hard, and therefore extra painful whenever I bashed into them. But I didn't care. I was on my way out of the forest and away from psycho Jack.

You're doing well, Ellen, I told myself. *That's it, just stay focussed. Keep going. You can do this.*

It was all going well for a while. Time meant nothing, I have no idea how long I was running for; it could have been minutes or hours. It was like I was having an out-of-body experience, nothing felt real anymore. I was the most focussed person in the universe, I was running towards safety. Every now and again, an owl hooted, making me jump. I was acutely aware of sounds, half-expecting Jack's footsteps to come upon me at any moment. But so far so good...

But then disaster struck, as I tumbled head first over a log that was hidden in the blackness of the night. The same ankle that I'd already injured took the brunt of the fall, and this time I bit my lip hard with the effort of not screaming out in pain. Shit. I couldn't get up, despite my best efforts. I was in another swampy hole, and this time I literally couldn't stand up on my ankle. I'd made too much noise when I'd fallen, I knew I had. It was like sending up a beacon, letting Jack know where I was. Stupid, stupid girl.

No, I screamed internally. *Please no.*

CHAPTER SIXTY-NINE

I'll have to stay very still, I decided. *And hope that Jack doesn't see me. Maybe he'll keep walking past me...* I knew that with my ankle now fucked, there was no point in running any more. I would make too much noise as I kept falling over, and there was no way I could now go on as fast as I had been...

'Ellen,' I heard Jack calling. There was a cajoling quality in his voice. 'Come on now. There's nowhere for you to go. Be a good girl and do your duty. Show yourself to me. God has a plan for you, Ellen.'

Fuck that, I thought, gingerly lying down as quietly as I could. Once I was horizontal on the forest floor, I rolled – slowly and carefully – to one side, until I was almost fully under a thick prickly bush. Shooting pains were now going from my ankle all the way up my leg, but I curled my limbs under the bush as best I could. Then I lay very still, and then for the first time in years, prayed to anyone who was listening to keep me safe.

But then I saw it. The light of a torch, sweeping over the undergrowth in front of me.

'Ellen?' Jack's voice again. This time he was sounding angry.

'I've had enough of your games. It's time to show yourself.' He was much closer to me now.

There was crunching and snapping, as his footsteps plodded over the undergrowth. Each sound was so clear to me, like it was happening in slow motion. I held my breath and waited. He'd clearly brought a torch with him in his stupid bag.

I stayed in that position, hardly daring to breathe, for a good few minutes. At one point Jack's voice got further away again, and a little ray of hope entered my brain. Maybe he wouldn't find me. It was a possibility, after all... I was shaking with cold now, as much as with fear. If Jack didn't finish me off then the elements might, but I couldn't think like that. I was just acutely focussed on staying alive.

Just hang on, I told myself. *Just stay with it, Ellen. You can do this.*

But as the sweeping torchlight came back, ending up almost right in front of where I was lying, my heart dropped.

'Ah, there you are,' Jack's voice said. His footsteps crunched until they were right in front of me. I could see his stupid trainers and the bottom of his jeans. I looked up and the bright light from his torch blinded me. 'You silly, silly girl.'

CHAPTER SEVENTY

'Why are you running, Ellen?' Jack sounded like he was forcing his words out through gritted teeth. 'Don't you know that sinners need to take their punishments with good grace? My father always told us that. He said you need to face what you have coming to you with a strong heart. Not run away from it.'

I continued to lie very still, like a rabbit in the road that's watching a car bombing towards it. I was frozen, caught. Trapped by my persecutor. The light from his torch was still blinding me, and I had no idea what to do. I'd run out of options. I was almost numb with cold. I was hurt. I'd tried my best to escape, I really had. I'd run as fast as I could under the difficult conditions that I was in, but it hadn't been good enough. My once beloved Jack, who'd turned out to be a psychopathic monster, was about to kill me. I felt my body relaxing as I accepted this fact. He was the only one making decisions now.

A strange peace descended over me, as I realised that I no longer had any control over what happened to me. My life was in Jack's hands now, and I knew he was planning to end it.

There was nothing more that I could do, and strangely, my mind seemed to accept that. It was flooded with peace, almost a euphoric feeling.

I shut my eyes...

CHAPTER SEVENTY-ONE

I t was at that minute that I heard the chopper flying above the trees. My eyes sprang open again.

Could they be looking for me? I wondered. *Oh God, I hope so. But they're too late now...*

I lay very still while Jack continued to berate me, the light of his torch constantly shining on to my face. He didn't seem bothered by the helicopter above us. Maybe he was so angry that he hadn't noticed it. Maybe his grandiose ego just didn't care. I know now that Jack's a narcissistic psychopath, one of the most dangerous. He truly is a most malevolent person. Perhaps he thought he could outwit everyone, including the emergency services, and that's why he ignored the loud sounds of the chopper. I closed my eyes again. It was over now. Even if the helicopter above me was out looking for Jack and I, he'd be able to finish me off before anyone found me. I hoped the end would be quick...

'Get up,' he said, reaching down and yanking my arm up roughly. 'Get up now, Ellen. I've had enough of your games.' The bag on his shoulder bashed into me.

'But the police are coming, Jack,' I said, as a bright white searchlight from the helicopter beamed down through the trees. For a minute, Jack and I and the whole scene around us were lit up, as though we were on a stage. 'You might as well make a run for it while you can, otherwise they'll find you.'

'I've got some business to finish here before I do that,' Jack said. 'Get up.'

In one movement, probably powered by his furious anger, he wrenched me up and grabbed me round the waist. It was then that I felt the thick rope that he was carrying in one of his hands. I could feel it brushing against my skin, course and rough. No doubt that had been in his bag of wonders, too. It was all so premeditated.

'Get over here,' he said, half dragging me towards a tree. He placed his torch on the ground, so that it shone a light on the tree, and then he slapped and then punched my face. 'This is all your fault, Ellen,' he said, as I staggered and fell. 'You stupid, meddling cow. You deserve to die, and my dad agrees with me. He says it's your time now, you need to leave this Earth and go to hell.'

He reached down and threw a noose over my neck, and pulled it tight. Then he threw the long end of the rope up and over a branch of the tree. I noticed that he was wearing gloves now, and even in my terrified state I realised that if he'd also worn some during the murder of his family it would explain the lack of his DNA at the crime scene.

'This is my trademark way of killing, after all,' he said as he heaved me upwards. 'Don't want to disappoint the coppers. They're still so confused about what happened to my family, bless their thick little heads.' The rope was squeezing my neck tighter and tighter. The pain and lack of air was making me lose consciousness. Everything was taking on a surreal quality. I could no longer see. I could hear myself gasping for breath, but it felt like someone else was making those noises. Not me, I was becoming separated from my body...

When I was suspended in the air with my feet dangling off the ground, Jack picked up the torch and shone it right in my face. He laughed.

'Now seems the right time to tell you that of course I know it's not my dad talking through me, you silly bitch,' he said. 'You were right. You wanted me to be honest with you, tell you the truth, so now I am. I don't actually believe in God anymore either. But you fucked everything up for me, and you more than deserve to die. They say that revenge is a dish best served cold, and it's fucking freezing out here tonight, so I guess I've achieved that one. Have a nice death, Ellen. Buried or hanging, you're still going to where you deserve to be.'

The last thing I remember hearing before the blackness washed over me and I began to die, was his pounding footsteps getting further and further away.

CHAPTER SEVENTY-TWO

Beeping around me. The smell of disinfectant. Murmuring voices. A sharp pain in my arm. Raging hot agony around my neck. The familiar scent of lavender soap...

I opened my eyes.

'Hello love,' my mum said. She was sitting in a chair next to my bed. She looked about twenty years older than usual, her face was so haggard and stressed. 'Welcome back. We thought we'd lost you there for a while.' She leaned forwards and kissed my forehead very gently.

'Where am I?' I said, looking around. I was in a cubicle; the beige flowery curtains were drawn shut. There was a shelf nearby that had an assortment of items on it, including a cardboard bowl, a box of disposable gloves and a row of bottles.

'You're in Milton Keynes Hospital again, Ellie,' my mum said. 'Jack tried to hurt you very badly, but the police found you just in time. That was two days ago, and you've been unconscious ever since. I've been with you all the time, talking and singing to you. I knew you'd open your eyes eventually.'

'By hurt, do you mean kill?' I said, attempting a faint smile.

My mum had always tried her hardest to protect me from the darkness in life. She didn't call the dead wild animals that occasionally lined the roads 'roadkill' like everybody else, she called them 'road sleepers'.

'Well, yes,' she said, tears springing to the corners of her eyes. 'Yes, that horrible boy tried to hang you in Salcey Forest, Ellen. You've been through so much, bless your heart. But you've survived it all, and I'm so, so proud of you.'

Ah, I thought. Jack tried to hang me. That would explain the burning pain around my neck. Now that I was waking up more, I realised that my whole body was in pain. Not just pain, it felt like I'd been on a medieval torture rack and had received the worst treatment possible. My neck was the worst, then my ankles, wrists, and pretty much everything else. Even my cheeks hurt. I cast my mind back, trying to remember the events that had led up to me lying here. But everything in my brain just felt comfortably hazy. It was as though it was in caring mode, and wouldn't let me access the bad bits just yet. Which was fine with me. Yes, I knew that Jack had turned out to be a bad apple. He'd lied to me about stuff. He was responsible for the deaths of his family. But other than that, everything was just a comfortable blur. *And long may it stay that way*, I thought.

'Well, you look very happy,' my mum said, giving me a watery smile. 'Must be all that morphine the doctors have got pumping into you.'

'I'm on morphine and my neck still hurts as badly as this?' I said. *Christ, what would it feel like when the painkillers wore off? Bastard Jack, making me go through all this.*

'Nala?' I said, suddenly remembering her. "Jenny?"

'Don't worry, Nala's been living with me,' Mum said, her tone soothing. 'She seems to rather like exploring my overgrown garden. I think she pretends that she's a tiger in the jungle, the way she pounces through the long grass. And Jenny is absolutely fine. She's just been worried about you, like all of us have.'

Then something dawned on me. Panic shot through me. My whole body went rigid. I tried – unsuccessfully – to sit up.

'Hey.' Mum stood up and enveloped me in a big hug. 'What's up, Ellie?'

'Jack?' I said. 'Has he been caught? Because if he hasn't...' I began looking about, half-expecting him to burst through the cubicle curtains. After all, I'd escaped from him once before, only to have him turn up and try to kill me...

'They've found him,' my mum said, stroking my hair. 'They've got him safely locked up, Ellie. You can properly relax now. You're safe, really safe. DS Moretti has come to the hospital every day, keeping me up to date with everything. They found Jack yesterday, hiding in an old World War Two bunker in Salcey Forest. He'd been digging a deep hole next to the bunker, and the police suspected it was probably intended for you, not that we would ever have allowed him to get near you ever again. He's behind bars now, and I very much doubt whether he'll ever be a free man again. You can put him out of your mind forever.'

She lifted up a newspaper, a copy of *The Buckingham Echo*. **Jack Bryant Caught at Last,** the headline shouted. I didn't need to read any more. Those five words told me everything that I needed to know.

'Good,' I said, leaning backwards again. 'At last.' So they'd finally found Jack. Thank fuck for that. For a while, I didn't think they ever would. That he was just one of those slippery eels who evaded the law. Turned out he wasn't as clever as he thought he was.

'Speaking of DS Moretti,' Mum said. 'I think I can hear his

voice now. He's been wanting to talk to you since his officers found you in the forest. He thinks you might be able to help him understand more about why Jack did what he did. Do you feel well enough to speak to him?'

CHAPTER SEVENTY-THREE

'Is it okay if I come in?' the detective's voice called. 'A nurse has just told me the good news, that Ellen has woken up. I'd love to see her, if I may?'

Mum looked at me, and I nodded.

'Yes,' she called back. 'Come in, Detective.'

DS Moretti parted the curtains, and beamed at me.

'Good to see you, Ellen,' he said. His smile was so genuine that I couldn't help giving him a grin back.

'I might take this opportunity to go and find myself a strong cup of coffee,' Mum said. She looked at me. 'Is that okay with you, Ellie? I won't be long. I've been gasping for one for a while now.'

I nodded, although I didn't really want her to go. But I knew she'd gone through a hell of a lot herself over the past few days, and she did love a cup of coffee at the best of times. There would be a lot of time for me to work on this co-dependence I now had on her. Now that Jack was locked up, and I was safe.

'That's fine,' I said. My voice sounded rather small.

'I'll take good care of her,' DS Moretti said in his deep voice, sitting down in the chair that Mum had just vacated. I watched as Mum walked through the curtains and disappeared. 'Now, young lady. Would it be all right if I asked you a few questions? I have a feeling that you have a very interesting story to tell me...'

CHAPTER SEVENTY-FOUR

I told the detective everything that I could remember. And as I talked, the protective film left my mind, and bit by bit, all the horrendous details returned. How Jack had put me in Jenny's car, and driven me to a forest. How I'd briefly escaped, how he'd found me, tried to hang me.

'And he said that of course he knew that his dad wasn't talking through him,' I explained, hot tears now pouring down my face, as the horror of everything that had happened radiated through me. 'Jack's not mad, he's evil. He's known exactly what he was doing the whole time.' I told him everything I could remember about what Jack had told me about the demise of his family members. How his mother and grandmother had almost willingly stepped on to the stools, ready to hang themselves. How he'd forced them all up at knifepoint. How Sabrina had caused him the most problems.

'Thank you, Ellen.' DS Moretti smiled. 'You're very brave. I'm so glad to have found you awake today; I have a very good feeling that you are going to make a good recovery. And in time, the bad memories of Jack will fade, I promise. You'll never forget what happened, but if you let it, this experience will make you stronger than you already are.'

Time for more tears to roll down my face. Jack. I'd been so in love with him. Had thought he was such a perfect specimen of a human being. How the hell had things come to this? I had to let go of being in love with someone. I'd really enjoyed that feeling, the tingles and the heart flutters that it had given me. But it had been based on a lie. I'd made up Jack's character in my brain, and it had blinded me to the real Jack – the evil, conniving man who'd used me. But I was smarter than that now. The euphoric feeling of being alive, that had come to me so strongly when I was trying to escape from him, was still there. It was like a strong energy pulsating through me, and I hope it never left. Now, it was just tempered with other emotions.

'I've got one more question for you, Ellen,' DS Moretti said. 'And then I'll leave you alone. Are you absolutely sure that Jack said he was writing down more instructions for his family in notebooks similar to the ones his father had used? Only, we've searched the whole house from top to bottom, and the only ones we found were the ones his dad had written. None with Jack's writing in them.'

'I'm absolutely positive,' I said, wiping my face. 'But then Jack's a liar isn't he? But he's also extremely manipulative. And it explains why he managed to get his whole family to hang themselves at the same time. He said that he told them that he was channelling his dead father, Dalton, from the other side. And that Dalton was calling the whole lot of them home, as they were failing in their duties and no longer deserved to live on this Earth. Jack's aunt, Marjorie, knew how brainwashed the whole family had become. But she failed to act. I strongly suspect that those notebooks do, or did, exist. But it wouldn't surprise me if Jack had destroyed them somehow. He was trying to make his father look like the only bully, and to portray himself as an innocent victim.'

A pang of anger stabbed through me, as I thought back to Marjorie sitting at her table, telling me how she'd known about Dalton's abuse, but had decided to do nothing about it.

'If only Marjorie had done something, the Bryant family could still be alive today.' I spat the words out.

DS Moretti nodded.

'I have to agree with you, Ellen,' he said. 'This whole case is extraordinary. I've never dealt with one quite like it before. It seems that Dalton, and then Jack after him, were pretty much running a family cult, with themselves as designated leaders. I've had experience of dealing with more organised cults before, but never with a family-run one. The extent of Dalton and Jack's power over everybody else is mind boggling. All except for Sabrina, who seemed so keen to escape from their clutches, the poor soul. The fact that Dalton and Jack stopped the rest of them from thinking for themselves, the fact that they became more and more isolated and afraid of telling the outside world what was going on at home, the enforced religiosity and metaphysical thinking, and the emphasis on obedience, first to the father, then to the brother, all points to cult-like behaviour in my experience. We now know that food was withheld from members of the family, and that they were sometimes physically, mentally and emotionally punished for their apparent 'sins'. From what I understand, Dalton had been getting increasingly financially abusive over Penelope, practically cutting off her access to money despite him hoarding a great deal, and Jack seemed to step into his father's shoes regarding this as soon as he could. His aunt Marjorie has told me all about how he would badger his mother for an early inheritance, which is why Marjorie stepped in and tried to look after the money so Jack couldn't get his hands on it. None of the children were allowed any independence, or to think about leaving the family or getting outside help. Only Jack left and came to live with you, and that's because by that point he'd turned from being one of the oppressed to being the new cult leader.'

I nodded, feeling tears wet my eyes. I was trying to take all of his words in. Yes, Jack had become the leader of his family cult. And the others had been too brainwashed by Dalton by that stage to know what to do about it. Dalton had done worse things than his own father, and Jack had done worse things than his. As Marjorie had said to me that day when I was having tea at her house; growing up in an abusive environment like that could make a person go one way or the other. And Jack had chosen to go into darkness; he'd chosen the bad path. And it was too bad about Sabrina. She was such a lovely person. And to think I'd envied her all those years, wanting to be her. Well, I didn't want to be anyone except for myself now. And when I was better, I was determined to be as 'me' as I possibly could...

The detective went on to tell me how they'd managed to find me in Salcey Forest. He explained that they'd used the trick that Jack had when he found me at Jenny's house in Grafton Regis. Using my mum's phone, they could easily find my location by tracking my phone – which was then in Jack's possession – and had immediately sent up a helicopter to help them with this. The pilot was able to give them the exact co-ordinates of where Jack was hanging me from a tree, and armed officers got to me after I'd passed out, and after Jack had made his escape. DS Moretti said that I was barely alive when they cut me down, and that no one was sure whether or not I was going to be able to pull through.

I nodded.

'But I did,' I said.

The detective smiled.

'There's also talk of getting Jack's father – Dalton's – body exhumed,' he said. 'We're no longer confident that he died from just a heart attack, given what a prolific killer – or attempted killer – his son turned out to be. So I'll keep you posted about that one.'

I nodded.

'Yes,' I said. 'Something Jack said makes me think you're right about that. He told me that his father had to go first. It sounds very much like he finished him off.'

The detective shot me an interested look, pulled out a notebook, and scribbled something down.

I suddenly felt extremely tired. My eyelids were closing...

'I'll leave you to rest now,' DS Moretti said. 'And thanks again, Ellen. You've been an absolute star. I'll be in touch...'

EPILOGUE
SIX MONTHS LATER...

'Are you off then, love?' Mum turned towards me as I walked through the kitchen. She'd done her hair nicely today, I noticed. I'd just finished a slice of buttery toast, and was wiping my mouth.

'Yeah,' I said, putting the napkin down and going over and giving her a big hug. Spending time in hospital and then convalescing at Mum's for a few months had given me time to reassess my life. This had been an eye-opening process. I'd realised that I didn't actually want to spend any more time on a sociology degree. My heart just wasn't in it. So when I was well enough, I'd spoken to the powers that be at the university, and managed to swap my course for another one. I wanted to study something that I did – now – feel very passionate about. Forensic psychology. I wanted to understand arseholes like Jack, find out what made them tick, and to eventually be able to work in the criminal justice system. I now got that there were some very dangerous people in the world, and I wanted to help treat them and help them and others to manage their behaviour, so that as few people as possible had to go through what I had at the hands of my ex-best friend. When I was accepted on to the forensic psychology degree course, it had been one of the proudest moments of my life. But not quite as good as surviving death, as beating Jack Bryant and living to tell the tale. Swapping my course had felt right, like I was now on the best path in life. Like it was meant to be.

Jack had been charged with my kidnapping and the attempted murder, and the murders of his six family members. Initially he'd denied the charges. Then, after his lawyer and him had come face to face with the endless evidence the police had collected – and my statements, plus my mum and Jenny's – he'd put in a plea of insanity. But after a psychologist had assessed him and found him to be compos mentis, he'd finally changed his plea to guilty. Which was a small bit of comfort in the whole horrible situation. I'd have to give evidence in court against him one day, but the date for that had yet to be set, so I wasn't going to worry about it. Coming face to face with him again wasn't going to be a problem, I'd already decided that. Because at the end of the day, I was going to walk out of that building a free woman, and he would hopefully never be set free again. I'd decided that I was never going to be scared of Jack again. He'd taken away my liberty when he'd kidnapped me those two times, he'd lied to me and pretended to be someone he wasn't. But I could see who he was very clearly now. And he didn't scare me at all. I just thought he was beyond pathetic, and I wasn't planning on ever wasting emotion on him again.

But I was still in the process of recovering from the whole ordeal. I was seeing a counsellor for trauma therapy once a week, and although she was really nice, I doubted whether I'd ever get over what Jack had done to me. The scars that the experience of being knocked out and shoved down the drain, and of being forced to go in the car with him, only to have him hang me, were too great.

Me and Nala were living full time at my mum's house,

there was no way I was ready to live alone again. And despite my best efforts, I hated Jack for taking my sense of independence away. But I had to look forward, not back. I knew that. And I appreciated being alive more than anything. I loved each fresh morning – I was often awake in the early hours – and I liked staring at the sky as dawn broke. And I was lucky, I knew. Luckier than poor Layla, anyway. She'd been brain damaged by Jack's frenzied attack on her; she'd never have a chance of getting back to being the girl she used to be. He'd hit her head too hard too many times. At least she was alive. Mum had met up with Layla's mother one day, as they wanted to chat as they'd both been through similar things. My mum seems stronger than she ever has done now. The experience of almost losing me must have sparked off hidden strengths in her. But she said that Layla's mum was broken, and I can understand why, poor woman. I've got the whole of my future in front of me now, but Jack has taken Layla's away, and unfortunately there's nothing anyone can do about that now.

I still woke up, sweating and screaming, in the middle of horrendously bad nightmares. Mum was like a patient angel, always coming into my room to see if I was okay on these occasions. I would have the deep scar around my neck forever, according to the doctors. They said that in the future I could always look at having a skin graft on it to hide it. But I was okay with the scar for now. It reminded me that I was a survivor, and that I'd been strong enough to outwit the psychopath who I'd once loved and been obsessed with.

When I was well enough, Mum showed me the pile of newspapers that she'd collected about Jack's crimes. **Local Girl Ellen Waldron Survives Bryant's Murderous Attack** I'd read, staring at the top one. I'd sifted through the stack of them, not wanting to read too much detail, but not minding that I'd been named as one of the people he'd tried to kill. The old Ellen would have hated that sort of media attention. But the new Ellen didn't mind, because I was proud of having survived, and it no longer bothered me if people stopped and stared, or tentatively asked me about what had happened. It had been Jack's sick mind that was the problem, I hadn't done anything wrong. I'd fallen in love with the wrong person, and I'd been way too trusting. But it had been Jack who'd done terrible things, not me. I was now firmly of the opinion that he should be feeling shame and humiliation. I didn't need to. I'd asked Mum to throw the papers away after I'd had a quick look at them. I didn't feel the need to keep any souvenirs from this episode in my life. The future was what mattered now, not the past. And definitely not Jack.

Today was the first day that I was going to walk to the university by myself. I'd only been back there for three weeks, and so far Mum had walked with me, right up to the door, each time I'd gone in. But yesterday, I'd decided that it was time for me to regain more control over my life. To become a pathetically dependent person forever was to let Jack win, and there was no way that I was going to let that happen.

I drew back and looked at Mum. She was desperately trying not to look worried. I knew she must be – she'd been through a hell of a lot too – but I also knew that she didn't want to hold me back. There were some very strange emotional struggles going on across her face.

'Bye,' I said. I wanted to make this big moment as casual as possible.

'Goodbye love,' she said.

We walked together to the front door.

'Ring me whenever you need to,' she blurted out.

I smiled.

'I will. I'll see you later, okay?'

'Okay.' She smiled, her shoulders relaxing a little. 'Have a good day, Ellie.'

As I walked down the pavement in the direction of the town centre, enjoying the feel of the late April sunshine on my face, I felt better than I had since the whole Jack incident. I was stronger now, I knew I was. I didn't trust people much anymore, and I never wanted to get obsessed with anyone ever again like I had with Jack. In fact, I didn't want to have a relationship with anyone for a very long time. But life was good. At least, it was getting better and better every day. Tom had come home for a visit, and had even given me a hug – before stealing my phone charger. I felt more 'me' than I ever had done before. And I was never going to give another thought to Jack Bryant; he could rot in his cell for the rest of his life, for all I cared. I was properly free from him now. And bloody hell, that felt good.

THE END

A NOTE FROM THE PUBLISHER

Thank you for reading this book. If you enjoyed it please do consider leaving a review on Amazon to help others find it too.

We hate typos. All of our books have been rigorously edited and proofread, but sometimes mistakes do slip through. If you have spotted a typo, please do let us know and we can get it amended within hours.

info@bloodhoundbooks.com

Printed in Great Britain
by Amazon

28624536R00139